D0564130

CHARM

Also available from

SARAH PINBOROUGH & TITAN BOOKS

Poison
Beauty

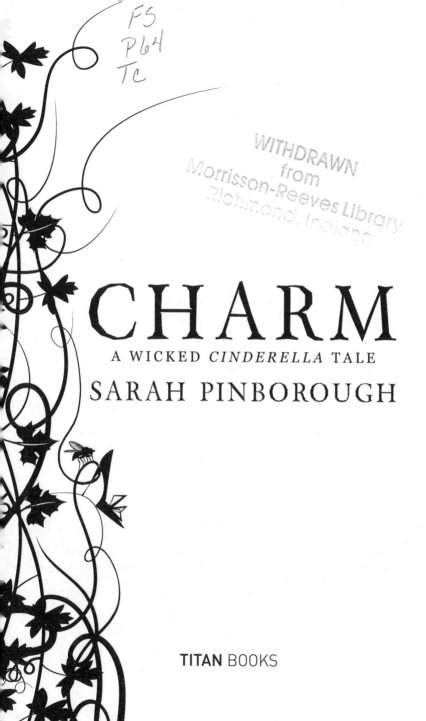

CHARM

A WICKED *CINDERELLA* TALE

SARAH PINBOROUGH

TITAN BOOKS

Charm
Print edition ISBN: 9781783291113
E-book edition ISBN: 9781783291137

Published by Titan Books
A division of Titan Publishing Group Ltd
144 Southwark Street, London SE1 0UP

First edition: April 2015
2 4 6 8 10 9 7 5 3 1

A CIP catalogue record for this title is available from the British Library.

Printed and bound in Spain.

FOR PHYLLIS, DI AND LINDY

1

'Once upon a time...'

Winter had come early. Its fierce breath tore the leaves from the trees before they had even turned crisp and golden, and although the New Year was still a month away the cityscape had been white for several weeks. Frost sparkled on window panes and the ground, especially at the cusp of dawn, was slippery underfoot. Only on those days when the sky turned clear blue, in a moment's respite from the grey that hung like a pall across the kingdom, could the peak of the Far Mountain be seen. But no one would really look for it until spring. Winter had come, and its freezing grip would keep the people's heads down until the ice melted. This was not the season for adventure or exploration.

As was the way with all the kingdoms, the forest lay

between the city and the mountain. It was a sea of white under a canopy of snow and, beyond the grasping skeletons of the weather beaten trees at its edge, it was still dense and dark. From time to time, on quiet nights, the cries of the winter wolves could be heard as they called to each other in the hunt.

The man kept his head down and his scarf pulled up over his nose as he moved from post to post, nailing the sheets of paper to the cold wood. It had been a particularly bitter night, and even though it was drawing close to breakfast time the air was still midnight blue. His breath poured so crystalline from his lungs that he could almost believe it was fairy dust. He hurried from one street lamp to the next eager to be done and home and by a warm fire.

He paused at the end of the street of houses and pulled a sheet of paper from the now mercifully small bundle tucked beneath his arm and began nailing it to the post. Residents would send their maids – for although these houses lacked the grandeur of those nearer the castle they were still respectably middle class, home to the heart of the city: the merchants and traders who kept the populace employed and alive – to discover what news there might be of the ordinary people. It wouldn't be spoken of when the criers came later to share news from the court.

Although he wore woollen gloves they were cut off at the knuckles to give his fingers dexterity, but after two hours in the cold the tips of his fingers were red and raw and clumsy. With the nail between his teeth he pulled the small hammer from his pocket but it tumbled to the ground. He cursed, muttering the words under his breath, and leaned forward, his back creaking, to pick it up.

'I'll get that for you.'

He turned, startled, to find a man in a battered crimson coat standing there. He had a heavy knapsack on his back and his boots were muddy and worn. He wore no scarf, but neither did he seem particularly bothered by the cold that consumed the city, despite the chapped patches on his cheeks. As the stranger crouched, the tip of a spindle was visible poking out of the heavy bag across his back.

'Thank 'ee.'

The stranger watched as he nailed the paper down, his eyes scanning the information there.

CHILD MISSING
LILA THE MILLER'S DAUGHTER
Ten years old. Blonde hair. Checked dress.
Last seen two days ago going for wood in the forest.

'That happen a lot?' The stranger's voice was light, softer than expected from his worn exterior.

'More than ought to, I suppose.' He didn't want to say too much. A city's secrets should stay its own. He sniffed.

'Easy for a child to get lost in a forest.'

'Easy for a forest to lose a child,' the stranger countered, gently. 'The forest moves when it wants, haven't you noticed? And it can spin you in a different direction and send you wherever it decides best.'

The man turned to look at the stranger again, more thoughtfully this time. The wisdom in his old bones told him that there were secrets and stories hidden in the weaver; perhaps some that never should be told, for once a story was told it could not be untold. 'If it's a man that's done it, then he'll take the Troll Road when they catch him, that's for sure.'

'The Troll Road?' The stranger's eyes narrowed. 'That doesn't sound like a good place.'

'Let's hope neither of us ever finds out.'

The barb of suspicion in the man's voice must have been clear, because the stranger smiled, his teeth so white and even they hinted at a life that was once much better than this one, and his eyes warmed. 'I did not see any children in the forest,' he said. 'If I had, I'd have sent them home.'

'Have you come far?' The man asked, putting his hammer back in his pocket.

'I'm just passing through.'

It wasn't an answer to the question, but it seemed to suffice and the two men nodded their farewells. Tired as he was, and with his nose starting to run again, he watched the stranger wander up the street with his spindle on his back.

The stranger didn't look back but continued his walk at a steady, even pace as if it were a warm summer's afternoon. The man watched him until he'd disappeared around the corner and then shivered. While he'd stood still the cold had crept under his clothes like a wraith and wormed its way into his bones. He was suddenly exhausted. It was time to go home. Around him the houses were slowly coming to life, curtains being drawn open like bleary eyelids and here and there lamps flickered on, mainly downstairs where fires were being prepared and breakfasts of hot porridge made. As if on cue, a door bolt was pulled back and a slim girl wrapped in a coat hurried out of a doorway and crouched beside the coal box with a bucket. Even in the gloom he could see that her long hair was a rich red; autumn leaves and dying sunsets caught in every curl.

The metal scraped loudly as she pulled the last coals from the bottom, the small shovel reaching for the tiniest broken pieces that might be hiding in the corners of the scuttle. There was barely enough in that bucket for one fire, and not a big one, the man reckoned. The girl would be going to the forest to fetch wood soon enough, missing children or not.

As she got to her feet their eyes met briefly and she gave him a half smile in return to his tug on his cap. He turned and headed on his way. He still had five notices to pin up and a smile from a pretty girl would only warm him for part way of that.

* * *

Cinderella was back in the house and clearing the ashes from the dining room fireplace when Rose came down in her thick dressing gown, her hands shoved deep in the pockets. Cinderella was dressed but she still hadn't taken her coat off. The house wasn't that much warmer than it was outside, and if they didn't start having fires in more than one room soon, she'd be spending her mornings scraping ice from the top of the milk and the morning washing bowls as well as doing all the other chores that had crept up on her over recent months, since Ivy's romance and wedding.

'It's getting colder,' Rose said. Cinderella didn't answer as her sister – her step-sister – pulled open the shutters and lit the lamp on the wall, keeping it down so low to preserve oil that it barely dispelled the darkness.

'So, what's the news?'

'What do you mean?' Cinderella finally looked up, her bucket of ashes full.

'I saw you reading the *Morning Post*,' Rose said, nodding towards the wooden post with the sheet of paper nailed to it and fluttering like a hooked fish in the sea of the rising winter wind.

'Another missing child. A little girl.' She got up and dusted her coat down. The new fire still needed to be laid but she'd forgotten to bring the kindling up from the kitchen with her.

She'd sit for five minutes by the stove and get warm first.

'Something needs to be done about whatever's in the woods,' Rose muttered. 'We can't keep losing children. And the forest is the city's life-blood. The more people fear going into it, the weaker the kingdom becomes.'

'Might just be winter wolves.'

'A sudden plague of them?' Rose's sarcasm was clear in both her tone of voice and the flashed look she sent Cinderella's way. 'It's not wolves. They can be vicious but not like this. And, without being indelicate, if it were wolves, at least some remains would be found. These children are disappearing entirely.'

'Maybe they'll turn up.' Cinderella was tired enough without having to listen to another of Rose's rants. She'd already put the porridge on, put the risen bread in the oven and after breakfast she'd have to peel the potatoes and vegetables before even having a wash.

'Of course they won't. And then we'll have a whole generation growing up scared to go into the woods and a society even more fuelled by suspicion. If the king doesn't act soon he's going to find the people losing their love for him. A visible presence of soldiers or guards at the forest's edge is what he needs. At the very least.'

Tight lines had formed around her mouth and between her eyes and Cinderella thought they made Rose look older than her twenty-five years. Rose's hair was fine and poker straight, the sort of hair that could never hold a curl for long, no matter how much lacquer was applied or how long the rollers were in, and although her features were regular enough there was nothing striking or unusual about them. She was, if the truth were to be told, a plain girl. Neither Rose nor her sister Ivy had ever been pretty. They might have come from money, but it was Cinderella who had the looks.

'Breakfast will be done in a minute.' She tucked a thick red curl behind one ear and picked up the bucket of ash. 'As soon as I've got this cleared away.'

'I'd help,' Rose said. 'But mother says I have to keep my hands soft.'

'Will take more than soft hands to get you wed,' Cinderella muttered under her breath as she headed for the door.

'What did you say?'

'A mouse!' The shriek was so loud and unexpected that Cinderella, whose arms were aching, jumped and dropped the bucket of ash, mainly down her own coat. 'There's a mouse!' her step-mother shrieked again, appearing in the doorway, her face pale and her hair still in rollers and firmly under a net from the night before. 'It's gone down to the kitchen! We can't have a mouse. Not here. Not now. Not with Ivy coming!'

'What is going on here today?' She stared in dismay at the cloud of ash that was settling across the floor and surfaces of her pride and joy, her dining room. 'Oh, Cinderella, we don't have time for this. Get it cleaned up. I want this place spotless by nine.' She turned to bustle away and then paused. 'No, I want it spotless by eight. And Rose, once you've had breakfast it's time for a facial and manicure. There's a girl coming at half past nine. Highly recommended.'

Cinderella looked down at her own chapped hands. 'I wouldn't mind a manicure.'

'Don't be so ridiculous,' her step-mother snapped. 'Why would you need one? Rose is the daughter of an Earl. People are beginning to remember that. And anyway, they're expensive, we can only afford one. Now come on, I want everything perfect for Ivy and the Viscount.' She swept out of the room, the mouse and the ash forgotten, and Rose followed her, leaving Cinderella standing in the pile of grey dust. She was living up to her name at least, she thought as she got down on her knees once more and reached for the pan and brush.

Ivy and her Viscount arrived just after noon, in a glorious carriage driven by two perfectly matching grey ponies. Cinderella watched from the window as her step-mother ran out to greet them, loitering perhaps a little longer than necessary in the freezing weather, in order to make sure all the neighbours saw her daughter's fine winter wolf stole and the rich blue of her dress. Cinderella thought she might kill for a dress like that, or even for a single ride in that beautiful carriage. Kill she might, but she wasn't sure she would kiss the Viscount for any of it.

She watched as Ivy took her new husband's arm and walked towards the house. Her pale face was rouged and her lips were painted pink and even her hair, almost as fine as Rose's, had managed to find some lift and body. Money was making her prettier, that was certain, but no amount of luxury could turn her into a beauty. Cinderella's stomach knotted in envy. It was all wasted on Ivy.

The Viscount was a nervous young man of perhaps thirty, whose right cheek had an unfortunate tic and whose shoulders hunched over slightly as if he didn't want to be noticed. He'd met Ivy when she'd run out in front of his carriage, chasing a note of money that was being blown across the road. By the time he'd picked her up, retrieved the money and driven her home, the two had somehow found something they liked about each other. Here they were, two months later, already married.

Cinderella watched as he sat quietly, smiling as his wife talked, not so dissimilar to her own father, who spent much of his time doing the same. The Viscount must love Ivy, though, she thought, otherwise how could he sit here and pretend that this small roast beef dinner was in any way satisfactory compared to the delicious feasts they must have at home every day? There wasn't even a girl to serve them

– other than Cinderella, of course – and despite the fire the room still carried a chill. She cut into her own tiny slice of beef, eating it slowly, just as her step-mother and father were doing, to try and prevent the Viscount from realising how much smaller their portions were than his or Ivy's. Thus far, it was working. He seemed perfectly content, but it was hard to know as Ivy was dominating the conversation.

'There are so many winter balls coming up, mama,' she said, her grey eyes alive with excitement and happiness. 'You've never seen anything like it.'

'Oh but I have, darling,' her mother countered. 'I remember my own coming out ball. I went to many balls as a young woman.' She smiled at the Viscount. 'I was quite the beauty then, you know.'

'Indeed you were, my dear,' Cinderella's father finally joined it. 'When I met you, you were quite breathtaking.'

His compliment earned him a sharp glance from his wife and Cinderella knew why. She didn't want the Viscount reminded of her fall from grace, not when she was so close to getting back into court society after all these years. The Viscount smiled anyway, and Cinderella noticed that the tic in his face had calmed in their company. She couldn't understand why, when their small house must be so far removed from the grandeur he was used to.

'Anyway, there is going to be one at the castle tomorrow night,' Ivy glanced at her husband and smiled, 'and George and I thought that perhaps you and Rose would like to come with us.'

The table erupted. Cinderella's step-mother was on her feet with her hand clamped over her mouth, but the shriek she was emitting behind it was loud enough to threaten their wine glasses. Ivy was smiling and laughing, and even the Viscount blushed slightly. Rose remained in her seat with her mouth half open, and then within seconds they were all talking over each other, a babble of excited chatter and plans.

Cinderella cleared away the plates. No one was going to eat any more after that announcement, and Cinderella was never going to go to a ball.

2

'He's a cheeky little fella, this one'

O nce Ivy and the Viscount had left, Cinderella retreated to the kitchen and busied herself with the washing up. For once she didn't care that much about being on her own downstairs. Her step-mother's excitement was too much for her to cope with. Tailors had been sent for and the last of the family coffers were being emptied in the search for ball dresses for Rose and her mother. There wouldn't be any coal for the foreseeable future, even if her father did sell a few more articles and papers or take in some bookkeeping while writing his interminable novel. Someone would have to go into the forest for wood, and that someone would no doubt be her. She shivered slightly at the thought. The forest was not the safest place to go wandering alone.

The kitchen, being in the basement, was at least warmer

than the rest of the house. And it was quiet. If she heard her step-mother squeal once more about the joys of court life she was sure she'd scream her self. All her own cries of 'but what about me?' had been ignored or brushed aside, as if the thought of her going to a court ball was such a ridiculous suggestion it wasn't even worth listening to. She finished the last of the dishes, placing the fine china carefully back in the cupboard where it would gather dust until Ivy and her husband came again, and then began to sweep the floor. She didn't hurry. Today she was glad of her chores.

There was a light tapping at the back door – three small knocks and then a pause before one more – and Cinderella's mood lifted. She pulled back the bolts and opened up, still smiling even though the blast of cold that rushed in threatened the tiny amount of warmth the room was managing to contain.

'Buttons!'

'Evening, princess.' He nodded at a brown sack by his feet. 'Shall I put it straight in the scuttle on my way back?'

'You've brought coal?'

'No one will miss it. They've got more than they need.' He grinned at her, dark eyes twinkling in the night. 'And we wouldn't want your pretty nose getting frostbite, would we? Speaking of frostbite, are you going to let me in?'

She ushered him inside and closed the door as he pulled another chair close to the stove and sat down. 'This winter's a bastard.' He shivered.

'You didn't need to bring me anything,' Cinderella rummaged in the cupboards, put some bread and cheese on a plate and poured him a glass of her father's table wine. 'You're too kind to me.'

'It's not my coal, princess. Just like the half a ham I just left at Granny Parker's wasn't my ham, so don't worry.' He winked at her. 'But I like bringing you things best.'

Cinderella blushed and sat down, happy to give him a moment or two of silence while he ate. Some times it felt like Buttons was her only real friend in the world, and she didn't even know his real name. She called him Buttons because he'd brought her two fine pearl buttons for her torn dress when she'd first met him and then the nickname stuck. He probably had grateful nicknames in houses all over the city. The winter made times hard, but Buttons made them better.

He couldn't be more than twenty or so, she thought. Thin and wiry with a mop of black hair and sharp eyes that were always up to mischief. But what a heart he had. She would never fall in love with him though, no matter how extraordinary he was. She wanted more from her life. She wanted what Ivy had, but with a tall, handsome man. She longed for it so much she ached from it.

'I hope you're careful,' she said. 'If you get caught, well...' She didn't need to finish the sentence. They both knew what the consequences would be.

Buttons was a thief. He was also an errand boy at the

castle and spent much of his time delivering messages to the great houses or doing chores in the castle itself. The latter fed into the former and Buttons was an expert at taking small but valuable items that no one would notice were gone and they would either be sold and the money given away, or he'd pass them on directly.

'I steal from the rich and give to the poor,' he'd told her once. 'It's the only way to be a happy thief. And so many people have so little while so few have so much. It's not fair.'

Buttons had made their winter easier, even if her family didn't notice. Why would they? It was Cinderella who did the day to day housekeeping and not even her step-mother had noticed they didn't have enough money for the food that was appearing on their table. But then her step-mother had never understood money – not until they'd run out of it, at any rate. She had been born in wealth and married in wealth and it was only when she'd run away with Cinderella's father she'd had to learn the cost of things. It appeared to have been a very long learning curve.

'Ah, there you are!' Buttons smiled as a small brown nose emerged from the warm gap between the oven and the tiles. He broke off a piece of cheese and held it out.

'Urgh, a mouse,' Cinderella pulled her feet up onto the chair. 'That must be the one all the fuss was about this morning.'

'He's a cheeky little fella this one,' Buttons said, as the mouse confidently ran towards him and sat up on his hind legs to take the offered chunk of cheddar. 'He's everywhere I go. Well, he was until last week. He must have followed me here and decided to stay.' The mouse didn't scurry back to his hiding place as Cinderella expected, but stayed where he was, settling down on his haunches and nibbling contentedly. 'I don't blame him,' Buttons said. 'He a mouse with good taste.'

'It's probably not even the same mouse. Mice don't follow people around.' She smiled. Sometimes with Buttons it was very hard to tell if he was joking or not.

'Oh, it's him. Look, he's got a little scar on his back. See?' He winked at her. 'Same mouse.'

'Well, I can't guarantee his safety if my step-mother finds him.' Cinderella slowly lowered her feet back to the ground. If it was Buttons' mouse then she was somehow less afraid of it. And there was something quite endearing about the way it was sitting between them, happily munching on the cheese.

'I think he's a hardy little fellow,' Buttons said. 'I know a survivor when I see one.'

'I hear there's a ball at the castle tomorrow night,' Cinderella suddenly blurted out. 'My step-sisters are both going. It's not fair.'

'Yes, yes there is. There are a few balls lined up I think. I've spent a lot of the day fetching polish and ordering the finest wines and foods to be delivered.'

'And the ballroom?' Cinderella asked. 'Are the chandeliers glittering? Will there be musicians?'

'You know all this,' he smiled, but his eyes were thoughtful. 'You ask me to tell you every time. But yes, it will be quite fantastic. There's a rumour that the Prince might be reaching the time when he wants to find a wife. If he does, he'll set a trend for all the young noblemen to marry. Where the prince leads, they follow.'

'Oh, how wonderful,' Cinderella said, taking a sip of Buttons' wine and then leaning back in her chair. 'Imagine how that must be, to have the prince fall in love with you.' Her voice had dropped to a slightly deeper tone, and Buttons raised an eyebrow. She smiled at him. This wasn't a new game, nor was it one they played often, but she needed an escape and Buttons was good at providing it.

'Can we?' she asked. She didn't need to elaborate. He smiled at her slightly and she smiled back. She didn't analyse their actions, and nor did she feel any guilt over it, even though no doubt her step-mother and father would be furious if they were caught. They weren't doing any real harm. It was just a game, and Cinderella was not the sort of girl to feel any shame over her body.

'Whatever you want, princess,' he said. 'What are friends for?'

Cinderella smiled and closed her eyes. They weren't hurting anyone. And they were friends, after all. As Buttons began to whisper to her, his breath warm in her ear, her drab surroundings were for gotten and she was transported to the castle, full of light and heat and beauty as couples danced around her and waiters moved elegantly between them with glasses of the finest champagne. She twirled from handsome man to handsome man in a dress of emerald green with jewels to match at her slim neck. Even the footmen at the doors couldn't take their eyes from her. In her fantasy – and it was one she had often – by the end of the evening she would have three men in love with her, all three ready to duel for her, and then the prince himself would sweep her away and marry her with more haste and urgency than even the Viscount for Ivy, and both her step-sisters would watch enviously as she lived happily ever after in the castle.

Buttons spoke softly of dancing and romance and, as she imagined the prince's body pressed close to hers, his hand slid up under her dress and his mouth softly kissed her neck. Her breathing came faster as finally, after teasing the soft skin of her thighs, his fingers hit their mark, teasing her to wetness and then sliding inside. She pushed against him and panted as he told her of beauty and music until eventually, her mind a whirl of ballrooms and the prince and music and love, she shuddered against his touch.

She sighed and lingered in her fantasy for a moment longer before opening her eyes and adjusting her dress and letting her miserable reality settle around her. 'It's so much better when you do it than me,' she said, and smiled, leaning forward and kissing Buttons' cheek.

'Oh you're a strange one, Cinderella,' Buttons' face had flushed slightly. 'There aren't many girls like you.'

'There are lots of girls worse than me,' she answered. 'It's only touching. What's wrong with that? It feels good. It's natural.'

'I'm not arguing with you,' he said. 'You're just full of contrasts.' He poured himself more wine. 'And rather me than another. I'm your friend. I'll never hurt you.'

'You're as strange as I am,' she said. Her comment didn't need an explanation, they both knew what she meant. She'd tried once, the first time they'd found themselves playing this game, to touch the boy. Not from any passion for him, but because she was curious and wanted him to feel as nice as she had, but he'd stopped her. He'd said that wasn't for him.

'That may well be true, princess.' He winked at her. 'That may well be true.'

She thought again of the castle and all its beauty and was quite envious that Buttons got to spend every day inside it.

'It must be wonderful,' she said. 'So much more wonderful than it is in my imagination. I would do anything to be part of that life. Anything at all.'

'Wonderful's one way to see it, I suppose.' Buttons finished his food and put the plate on the floor. The mouse scurried over and began sniffing for crumbs. Cinderella made a mental note to give that plate to Rose tomorrow at breakfast. Maybe it would make her sick and she wouldn't be able to go to the ball. It was a mean thought, but she couldn't help it.

'Of course it's beautiful,' Buttons continued. 'Beauty is easy with money and these people have the finest of everything.' He looked at her intently. 'But court life isn't all dancing and music and love, Cinderella. The gentle don't survive well when everyone is after power. Everyone is using other people to shuffle into a position where they have the king or the prince's ear. It's a place full of wolves in disguise. Why do you think I feel no guilt stealing from most of these people?'

Cinderella didn't say anything. She didn't care about all that and it wouldn't matter to her anyway. She had no interest in power, she just wanted beautiful clothes and music and fun. Life had been hard enough over recent years.

'Tell me again about their carriages,' she said, eagerly. 'The gold and silver ones. The king and queen's one that never leaves the castle gates because it's so encrusted with jewels they fear the ordinary people won't be able to stop themselves tearing it apart to have a piece for themselves. Tell me about that.'

She smiled at him, and this time it was his turn to sigh. 'They keep it in a converted stable at the back of the castle. It's under constant guard. At night it twinkles as though all the stars in the sky have been captured and sprinkled onto its surface...'

Cinderella closed her eyes and let her mind drift as the familiar words washed over her.

Buttons left an hour or so later, tipping the coal into the scuttle on his way, and taking the sack away with him to hide somewhere on his way back to the castle. The night had turned bitter, but Cinderella came up the outside stairs in just her worn shoes and with a shawl wrapped round her shoulders and watched until he'd vanished in the foggy mist that was settling over the streets like a blanket.

She didn't notice the little mouse valiantly scrabbling his way up the stairs, his fur puffed out a little as if it could somehow protect him from the grip of the icy night. By the time Cinderella had retreated back into the house and firmly bolted the door behind her, he had reached the pavement. He stood up on his hind legs and sniffed the wet air, searching for the right direction.

This time he didn't follow Buttons back to the castle, he turned away and scurried through the night towards the forest. He was glad he'd had the cheese and breadcrumbs. He had a long way to travel that night.

Cinderella had done her best to hide away for most of the next day – even going out for a long walk in the bitter cold –

but she'd still been subjected to having to 'ooh' and 'aah' at Rose in her new blue dress. Admittedly, she did look prettier in it. Her skin looked less pasty with some rouge applied and the royal blue made her hair look darker. It was even managing to hold some curls, although Cinderella doubted they would last. Doubted and hoped not, if she was honest.

By the time Ivy's carriage arrived, she was in a foul mood. She watched through the window as a footman helped Rose and her step-mother inside, her mind a nest of squirming dark feelings that she couldn't even form into coherent thoughts. It was envy of course, she knew that. Envy and more than a touch of self pity, but she couldn't help herself. How was she supposed to feel? It just wasn't fair. It was as if she didn't matter.

'Penny for them?'

The carriage rolled away and Cinderella let the curtain drop.

'Doesn't matter.'

'Your mother got these for you.' Her father was standing in the doorway holding up a box of chocolates. 'It's a two-layer box. Not cheap.'

'I don't want them.' She almost stamped her foot, the way she had when she was annoyed as a small girl. How could a box of chocolates compare with going to a ball at the castle? Was she being laughed at now? It felt like salt in a wound. 'And she's not my mother.'

'She's looked after you since you were very small, Cinderella. She loves you.' He'd been carrying a chequers board under his arm and he set it down on a coffee table and drew it close to the fire Cinderella had made with some of the coal Buttons had brought. It was a good fire and neither her step-mother or step-sister would feel the benefit of it. A small victory maybe, but it was something.

'You're not writing tonight?' she asked.

'I thought we'd have some father and daughter time,' he smiled at her. 'Eat some chocolate and play a few board games. What do you think?'

'I think I'd rather be at the ball, but my *mother* didn't invite me.'

Her father sighed and in the glow of the fire she noticed, for the first time, that more of his hair was grey than brown, and wrinkles ran like a spider's web across his face. How did that happen? He was suddenly middle-aged, not the smiling, solid man who'd bounced her on his knee when her real mother was still alive.

'You have a lot to learn, Cinderella. It's not so easy as that.'

'She hates me.' She flopped down into the chair opposite him, feeling more ten than twenty. 'She always has.'

Her father burst out laughing. 'Don't be so childish!'

She glared at him – probably childishly.

'Your step-mother, well, she feels a great responsibility for what her daughters lost. For what she lost. You were too young to understand. When she left the old earl and married me their entire lives changed. And does she miss the trappings of her old life sometimes? Of course she does. I could never give her all the things she used to have. Things she'd had all her life.' He gazed into the flames. 'But she chose us, Cinderella. Over all of that. And she never looked back.'

'You make it sound like true love.' Cinderella snorted; it was a ridiculous thought. 'If my mother hadn't died, you wouldn't have *needed* her.'

'Oh darling,' he smiled at her softly. 'It was true love. It *is* true love. You were too young to remember it all properly. Your mother – well, she could be difficult. If she hadn't fallen sick then I would have left her for Esme, just like Esme left the Earl for me.'

Cinderella stared at him as cold crept up from the pit of her stomach and burned her cheeks like ice. He couldn't mean that. He just couldn't. 'You're lying.'

Her father shook his head. 'No. It's true. It was true love. I was just the old Earl's secretary, but she fell in love with me and I with her. If you're lucky you'll find the same thing one day.'

'Not without going to a ball, I won't!' She got to her feet, tears stinging the back of her eyes. How could he have fallen in love with her stupid step-mother? How could he say her mother was *difficult*? True, she didn't remember her much, most of her early memories seem to just feature her father and flashes of a woman holding her close and reading her stories, but she was her *mother*. 'You're as bad as she is!'

She stormed out and stomped up the stairs, leaving the warmth of the fire and the chocolates behind her. She slammed her bedroom door and flopped down on her bed. A few moments later her father knocked on the door but she told him to just 'Go away!' before burying her face in her pillow and crying. She wasn't quite sure who she was crying for, but she knew she was completely alone. Not even her father was on her side. It wasn't fair. None of it was fair.

She must have eventually cried herself to sleep, because the next thing she knew, she was freezing cold on her bed and lights were being carried through the hallway, slivers of yellow moving and creeping under her bedroom door. There was a flurry of activity in the hallway; then feet coming up the stairs and her step-mother's laughter, loud and brash, dancing up ahead of them.

They were back.

Cinderella wrapped her shawl around her and lit the candle by her bed as if that small flame could give some heat as well as light, and then crept over to the door. She didn't want to face them and be drawn into conversation, but she did want to hear what they were saying. She hoped it had gone badly for them. After all, her step-mother had shamed the old Earl she'd wed by walking out on him, and although he'd died two years ago it was likely she still wouldn't be

welcome in the court circles. Even being the daughter of a
lord was no shield against scandal. The sound of merry, tired
giggles, however, put paid to that hope. Cinderella looked at
the clock on the wall. It was just after half past one.

'Oh, Rose. How wonderful.' Her step-mother had reached
the top of the stairs and Cinderella carefully pulled her door
open a fraction to hear them more clearly. 'You danced with
two Earls. Two. Can you believe it?'

'It didn't *mean* anything. It was just dancing.' Rose was
quieter, still down in the hallway. 'Oh, it's good to get these
shoes off. They're killing my feet.'

'And the prince kissed your hand!'

'I think he kissed everyone's hand.' Rose's voice was
full of good humour. She didn't sound like Rose at all. Then
her feet thumped up the stairs. *That* sounded like Rose; she
didn't have an ounce of grace in her clumsy body.

'But isn't he handsome, Rose? I mean, I knew him of
course, when he was a boy and he always had something
about him, but well...'

'Yes, he's very handsome. Now, please, please, please
help me get this dress off before my ribs break. I told you it
was too small.'

'Men like a slim waist, Rose. And, unfortunately, you're
rather too fond of food.'

Their voices faded and then there was the click of a door
closing as the two women disappeared into her step-sister's

room. Cinderella waited until there was only silence and then pushed her door shut. Her blood raced through her veins, the cold and her tiredness sloughed off as she absorbed what she'd heard. Two earls. And the Prince had kissed Rose's hand.

She picked up the framed print of the smiling Prince that she kept in her room – the picture Rose had once laughed at her for, even though nearly all the girls in the kingdom had one – and climbed into her bed, pulling the covers up to her chin. She stared at the handsome smiling face. How could he have kissed Rose's hand? It must have just been politeness. Yes, that was it. He'd kissed all the girls' hands, isn't that what they'd said? There was nothing special about Rose.

She blew the candle out and lay back on her pillow, the picture face down on her chest, and tried to calm down. Yes, she hated that Rose had gone to the castle when she hadn't, but maybe tonight's ball going well wasn't such a bad thing. Maybe if Rose got married off to some horrible old Earl like her mother had been, then surely their family would be respected enough for her to be invited? Just once. Just once. How she wished for it.

She closed her eyes and let her mind drift into the familiar fantasy.

She's standing in the castle and the ballroom is full of men and women dressed in their finery. As her name is announced at the top of the stairs, all eyes turn her way, and although no one knows who she is, they're dazzled by her style and beauty. She dances with the most handsome men, but all the while her eyes are locked with the Prince's until eventually he comes to claim her as his own. As they whirl around the room, they only have eyes for each other and she knows that he'll love her forever and she'll love him forever and they'll never stray. The music slows and he pulls her closer, his strong arm tight across her back. She can feel his body heat and every inch of her skin is aching for him to kiss her. Eventually, he does. His lips brush hers, teasing her until she can barely breathe and then his tongue touches hers and stars explode in her head.

Her fantasy shifted, as it always did, and it was their wedding night. The party was over, although in the streets it would continue for hours, and they had retired to their bedchamber. He was standing close to her, his lust so clear in his hazy eyes, and his hands undid the strings of her shift leaving her naked before him. Her hand slipped into her night dress and teased her right nipple as if it was his fingers and then mouth. She gasped slightly, lost in the moment, her head filled with experiences she could only imagine. His hand in her hair as he kissed her. Her arms wrapped around his neck as he pushed her to the bed. Feeling him pressing against her as they lost themselves in their passion. Her hand moved further down, sliding between her legs and exploring the wetness there.

Her hand was his hand, and then, as her own touch

moved into a rhythm, he was inside her, moving with her, his mouth on her neck, his own moans coming louder, her arms over her head and pinned down by his hand as he possessed her. They moved like frantic animals, growing rougher with each other as their needs grew more urgent until finally, in her small bed in the merchant's house, Cinderella's back arched and the stars exploded bright behind her closed eyes.

3

'A Bride Ball...'

'Their boy's gone missing in the woods.'

'The baker's boy? Jack?'

'They didn't send him alone, did they?'

'No, young Greta was with him. She came back. She must have had a fever though, because she was full of wild stories.'

Cinderella was on the edge of the huddle out side the tiny store where a tired, red eyed man had just sold her a small loaf. She'd wondered why he hadn't given her a wink and a smile as normal, but she'd just put it down to the terrible cold that rushed in every time a new customer opened the door and the fact that she wasn't in the best of moods herself and maybe that showed. But now she knew and the icy wind was nothing to the cold at the pit of her stomach. Jack was a good boy. He had his father's cheerful disposition and worked hard. Nothing bad could have happened to Jack? Surely not.

She listened to the low chattering voices around her.

'What do you mean, "wild stories"?'

'Well,' the old woman leaned in closer and her friends did the same. Standing just behind them, Cinderella couldn't help but feel that the subject of their conversation was obvious to the poor grief-stricken man on the other side of the window. But still she stepped a little closer too, in order to hear them.

'It was preposterous. Obviously she just couldn't cope with whatever had really happened, but she said that they'd stayed on the normal path, just like they'd been told to and just like they'd always done, but that the woods had moved somehow – the path had changed – and then before she knew it they were lost in the dense trees. They walked through the night—'

'But that can't be right!' a thin woman with a crooked nose cut in. 'She was back within a few hours, that's what my Jeannie told me and she lives near Greta's family.'

'Like I said, she must've had a fever or something. But this is the story she *told*, and that's the one you wanted to hear. Right?'

'Well, yes...'

'Then be quiet and listen.' The speaker pulled her shawl tighter round her shoulders and sniffed before continuing.

'So, they walked through the night and then they found this clearing. Right in the centre of it is a house. Made of cakes and candy according to Greta.'

A few snorts of derision accompanied this but any thought of laughter died with the next words. 'There was an old lady there. She invited them inside. Greta said no, but Jack went in. When he didn't come out, Greta went round to the back of the house to see if there was a window with the curtains open that she could see through.'

'What did she see?' They might have laughed originally but, just like Cinderella, the old women were being drawn into the story.

'Nothing. She saw what was piled up at the back of the house and she turned and ran back into the woods. She said she ran and ran until somehow she found her way back to the path.'

'Don't be a tease, Gertrude. It's freezing out here. What did she see?'

'Bones,' the woman's voice had dropped to a whisper. 'Small bones. Children's bones.'

There was a long pause after that.

'Pah,' the thin woman said, eventually. 'The boy got eaten by wolves and the girl got a fever. That's what that will be.'

'They need to do something about those woods.' The words were out almost before Cinderella knew she was speaking. 'They need more soldiers guarding them. We can't have a whole generation of children growing up scared to go into the woods. We need the woods.' She was repeating what Rose had said even though when her step-sister had spoken, Cinderella had been bored by it. But now she knew one of the children who'd vanished and that made everything different. Rose's words, much as it irked her, made sense. The three women turned to stare at her.

'It's true,' Cinderella stammered on. 'Someone needs to talk to the king about—'

Her sentence was cut off by the thunder of horses' hooves and the burst of a herald's horn as the two men in livery clattered into the street. She stared at them. The Royal Crier? The baker's boy and his terrible fate were forgotten, and even the baker came out to join the throng who hurried to gather and hear the castle news. Royal Criers were rare in this part of the city – not enough noblemen lived here – so whatever the news was, it would be of some great importance.

Cinderella pushed her way to the front of the growing crowd.

'Hear ye! Hear ye!' The young man on the white horse was wearing a tunic of red and gold without a speck of dust on it, and his perfectly styled brown hair shone almost as brightly as the leather of his riding boots. 'His Majesty the King announces his intent to hold two Bride Balls two weeks from Saturday for his royal Highness the Prince. All young ladies of noble birth and their chaperones are invited to attend. The Prince himself will dance with each, and by the end of the two balls he will have selected his bride.'

A rush of gasps and excited babble ran through the crowd as women and children clapped their hands together excitedly and men smiled and slapped each other on the back. A royal wedding meant extra holidays and feasting and the king could be very generous when he wanted the people to celebrate with him. Pigs would roast on street corners and ale would flow. There were good times ahead.

Cinderella almost dropped the shopping she carried. The prince was having two Bride Balls and she wouldn't be invited. *She* wouldn't be, but Rose and her step-mother would. It was so awful she couldn't bear it. Worse still, she was going to have to put up with hearing about it for the next two weeks. As if reading her mood, the sky darkened, and as she reluctantly hurried home an icy rain began to fall.

Steps were hard to manage when you were a mouse and it took him two whole days and nights to reach the top of the castle tower. It was a long, long way up at the end of an already long journey and he was exhausted. At least the forest had been kind and given him a clear path and the leafy canopy had protected him from the cold nights. A hare had carried him part of the way, letting him sleep in the warm fur of its back as it bounded through the night and he wondered once again at magic and nature and fate and how bound together they all were in the forest.

He had been surprised by the city. The first clues that all was not well had come when he passed the mines. The songs that hummed in the air, as if the mountain itself was singing, were melancholy and ached with tiredness. The hardy dwarves were finding no pleasure in their toil. At the edge of the woods were patches of dead ground as if the bushes and trees which had grown there had simply given up and slumped into a pile of rotting mulch.

It was winter across all the kingdoms, and those in the East were always gripped harder and for longer than the rest, but he had not expected what he found here. Black ice was slick across the tracks and roads and the sky raged in grey and ragged darkness whatever the hour of the day. Ravens covered the rooftops.

He had kept close to the buildings as his tiny feet carried him, fast as they could, towards the castle at the city's core. It grew colder with each step and the wind blew harder. The castle, it soon became clear to him, was the eye of the storm. This was an unhappy city, a bitter sadness spreading like a pool of blood from the wound at its heart.

It was also a city in mourning. In each house he passed colourful drapes had been removed and replaced with the customary black, and all were pulled shut. Many shops were closed, only those selling the necessities of life allowed to trade, but still their windows had been blackened and there were no cheery greetings or hawking of wares.

The little mouse paused in his quest and squeezed through a gap in the wall of a house, eavesdropping in the warm for a while and, as well as stealing a few breadcrumbs from the floor, he learned what had passed.

The king had died in battle. His body had not yet been returned home.

It did not come as a surprise to the mouse. Kings liked battles and brave kings often got in the midst of them. And in the midst of every battle sat death, making his camp in the melee and gorging on life until his hunger was sated. All life was equal. Kings died as easily as other men.

So now the queen and her magic were in charge, and although the woman who chattered as she sewed seemed convinced that the winter storm was just the icy queen's expression of grief for her lost husband and vanished step-daughter, the mouse thought that perhaps the rest of the city was not so kind in its judgements. They thought perhaps, as could be seen in the nervous glances up at the ravens, that the queen was not so sad her husband would no longer be returning to her bed. That the queen had what she'd always wanted; a kingdom of her own. None of the nobles would challenge her rule, even though, by the laws of the land, they had every right to. Magic and bitterness could be a terrifying combination. Kings might die in battles but politicians chose theirs more wisely. This second wife was not to be challenged lightly.

She didn't see him for a while. She was lost in her reverie, her knees pulled up under her chin, curled up in the single throne at the centre of the tower. Around her the life of the city so far below played out in the mirrors, the bewitched ravens' eyes showing her everything they saw. She wasn't looking though. Her beautiful face was dark and drawn and lost in places that belonged only to her.

He squeaked.

She jumped.

She swore under her breath, a crude word entirely out of place in one so high in society, and raised her hand. Sparks glittered at her fingertips and then she paused and frowned, leaning forward to take a closer look. He stood up on his hind legs as she loomed over him, her pale face an enormous moon against the black night of the walls that were fractured with red lightning. There were fresh lines around her eyes and her cheekbones were sharper. But then, he thought, and if a mouse could smile he would have, they'd both changed since he'd taken her on this cool marble floor.

She stared at him for quite a while and he stared back. He was banking on her curiosity getting the better of her, rather than destroying him at her feet. His future happiness as well as his life depended on it. Finally, her fingers sparkled *again and a tinkling sound filled the air as the glittering light coated him with its warmth, and the world shimmered and shook and trembled and so did his insides.*

He was a man again.

He was also dressed, which came as something of a relief. For a moment he felt quite dizzy, strange to be tall in the world after such a long time, and there was a strange sensation in his gut which let him know he wasn't free of her curse but had only a temporary reprieve.

He did not waste time flirting with her. Whatever moment of lust they had once shared was long gone for both of them. Instead, she poured two glasses of wine and they sat on cushions on the floor and talked long into the night. Finally a pact was made, an agreement of sorts, and she told him how his curse could be lifted. It was the way of all curses and it came as no surprise. Until then, however, she would half lift it so they could help each other. As deals went, it could have been worse.

It was only when morning came and he was a mouse again did he wish he'd thought to go back down all the stairs before the change had been once again upon him.

It was a long two weeks between the announcement and the commencement of the Bride Ball, and throughout the city there was an air of excitement, even among the common people who would never in their lifetimes get through the castle gates. All day long dressmakers hurried from one noble house to another, each trying to come up with unique designs that would guarantee to catch the prince's eye and his heart. No expenses were being spared and the tradesmen were happy. Jewellers, hairdressers and haberdashers were bringing the sinking economy back to life and butchers and bakers were also busy, as many of those who had no chance of a royal invitation planned their own parties at home. Bride Balls were a rarity and everyone wanted to enjoy the weekend of festivities.

Except perhaps Cinderella. The days dragged by endlessly as teams of experts traipsed in and out of the house. There was a woman to teach Rose deportment, there was another to manage her eating as her mother insisted she must lose several pounds if she was to shine and not look like a 'brood mare' compared to the glamorous young ladies of the court. A man came to teach her how to engage in court conversation, another how to dance all the latest fashionable reels. They arrived like an army before it was light and they often kept working her until it was very nearly midnight.

Cinderella moved quietly around the house doing her chores but all the time watching and learning. Alone in her room she'd easily manage the moves Rose found so difficult, twirling this way and that, so naturally elegant compared to the girl who spent most of her afternoons thudding across the floor, trying to dance in the heels she'd been bought especially to practise in. It wasn't fair, Cinderella would think, for the hundred thousandth time. It just wasn't fair. She almost wept with envy when the dressmaker came bearing swathes of beautiful silks for Rose to choose from. Ivy was paying for her sister's dress and cost was no object, and her mother was holding her to that.

Rose was pinched and pinned and squeezed and tutted at until two suitable designs were chosen and then the exhausted girl was sent to bed with no supper in order that she might just fit into her gowns by the night of the first ball. Cinderella heard her sobbing through the wall one night and almost knocked on the door but decided against it. What could she say? Rose knew how much Cinderella wanted that invite herself. She could hardly pity her step-sister for being the one allowed to go. But still, though she might be terribly, achingly jealous of the event, she was no longer jealous of Rose.

The preparations were endless and her step-mother had become relentless in her determination to turn her daughter into a girl to rival those of the best houses of the kingdom. Cinderella wondered if perhaps, underneath all the laughter and reminiscing of her youth, that first ball hadn't been too kind to her. Had she been the subject of a few barbed remarks she hadn't told Rose about? Did she have a few scores to settle at the castle?

For the first time Cinderella gave some proper thought

to her step-mother's life *before* this one. How very different it must have been. And how very difficult it must have been to go back into that castle where so many people would remember what she'd done. It made Cinderella feel strange. She didn't want to feel sorry for either her step-mother or Rose, but somehow she did. Her step-mother had become obsessed with regaining her place in court life and Ivy and the Viscount weren't enough. The Viscount was a nervous man and preferred to spend his time with his new wife in the privacy of their estate rather than wrangling in court matters, and so now all her hopes were pinned on Rose to secure her position.

'If you can make the prince fall in love with you, Rose, just imagine...'

Cinderella had lost count of the times she'd heard those words from her step-mother by the time the night of the first ball finally drew close. There was an edge to it. A nervous anxiety. Cinderella might want to go to the ball, yes, but she was very glad she wasn't Rose. Rose was exhausted and her step-mother was on the verge of madness as far as she could see. It must be madness if she thought a man as wonderful as the prince would ever think of marrying a lump like Rose. It was impossible. And Rose, Cinderella suspected, knew it.

4

'All beauty is magic'

On the opening night of the Prince's Bride Ball the thick grey clouds that had coated the kingdom throughout winter cleared and the curious sky looked down on the magical proceedings occupying the city so far below. The stars sparkled like diamonds on a midnight blue dress and the bitter wind dropped, as if nature itself didn't wish to damage the carefully styled curls that had taken hours of primping and preparation.

The frantic atmosphere that had gripped the city for the previous two weeks finally eased into happy excitement. The dress fittings were all done. The carriages were booked. The moment the ladies of the land had been waiting for was finally here. Tonight, they would all dance with the prince, and by the end of the next Ball one of them would return home engaged. Although each girl protested aloud that of *course* he wouldn't choose them, in their hearts they hoped and hoped he would.

All the starving had worked and Rose's crimson dress fitted perfectly. Rose Red, her step-mother had called her, smiling proudly at the culmination of all her hard work. Cinderella didn't say anything, but she had to admit that Rose looked quite pretty. If not beautiful, then perhaps intriguing and elegant. Her step-mother wore a dress of chaperone brown as was the custom, but it was rich taffeta and the colour suited her. Cinderella watched them from the doorway of the sitting room as they waited in the hallway to leave, and she had never felt more like a poor secretary's daughter.

Her father, standing on the stairs, caught her eye and smiled at her, but she ignored him, and slunk past them all and down to the kitchen. Her father would say she was sulking, and perhaps she was, but he would never understand. How could he? Ever since the newspaper had been shut down, his ambitions only went as far as writing his stupid novel or stories or whatever it was he did locked away in his attic study all day. He didn't care about visiting the castle or fine clothes and dancing. How could he possibly understand how unfair all of this felt to her? But then, what did she expect? He'd already said he'd have left her poor mother for that silly cow of a step-mother if she hadn't died. He was as horrible and selfish as the rest of them. He should be on the outside, like her, not approving of all the spending that had taken place just so Rose could go to a ball that would come to nothing and leave them all in debt.

She opened the back door and crept out onto the steps leading from the basement to the pavement level. Frost bit in the air, but without the sharp wind the night was comparatively mild, and she sat on the cold, damp stone and watched as Ivy's beautiful carriage pulled up and Rose and her step-mother, their hands warm in fur stoles that matched the elegant wraps over their shoulders came out, laughing, and climbed aboard.

Cinderella stayed on the step long after the carriage had carried them away to the castle, staring up at the night sky and fighting back tears. Was this how her life was going to be forever? Always in drudgery, working in the shadow of Rose and Ivy? The poor step-sister? The commoner? Maybe that was how it had to be, but all she wanted was one night. One night of feeling special. Overhead, a star shot across the dark sky. She squeezed her eyes shut. Just one ball, she wished. If only she could go to the castle just once.

'It would appear I'm late.'

Startled, Cinderella opened her eyes, just in time to see the last of the sparkles of light disappear in the frosty air, leaving a beautiful woman in their place. Her blonde hair, so light it was almost the colour of ice, ran freely down her back and against her black dress her skin was pale. Her blue eyes were like frozen pools. She tucked the black wand she carried into a velvet bag and glanced, irritated, down at a small brown mouse who sat at the hem of her gown. 'The directions weren't the best.'

'Who are you?' Cinderella breathed. The woman had appeared out of nowhere in a flurry of what could only be magic. What was she doing here?

'I suppose,' the woman shrugged, 'if you must call me something, you can think of me as your fairy godmother. Now let's get inside. It's bloody freezing out here and I need something to drink.' She shooed the mouse away so it scurried round the corner of the building and then glared at Cinderella. 'Well, come on then. Do you want to go to this ball or not?'

Inside the warmth of the kitchen Cinderella thought her fairy godmother looked even more beautiful than she had in the moonlight. Her delicate features were catlike but there was a hardness in her poise that transformed her into something ethereal. There was also something quite unsettling about her. She hardly radiated kindness. She was yet to even smile.

'This is the best you have?' she asked Cinderella, frowning slightly as she swallowed a large mouthful of red wine.

'I'm sorry, yes. We're not... we don't have much—'

'It will have to do then.' The fairy godmother leaned back on the kitchen table and studied Cinderella thoughtfully as she refilled her glass. 'So, you want to go to this Prince's Ball?'

'Oh yes,' Cinderella's eyes widened and her heart thumped. 'More than anything.'

'Let me guess. You want to dance with the prince, have him fall in love with you and then live happily ever after?'

'Oh yes.' Cinderella nodded eagerly.

'That I can't promise.' She drank some more wine. 'No amount of magic can guarantee you happy ever after. I can, however, guarantee you'll get his attention. Make him want you. You'll catch your prince. After that, though, all bets are off.'

'But how? How can I go?' Cinderella's head was in a whirl. She had dreamed so many times of going to the castle but she had never really thought it could come true. Was she dreaming? Was that it? Had she fallen asleep on the steps? 'I don't even have a dress.'

'Stop simpering.' Her fairy godmother's lips tightened. 'That part is easy.' She pulled a dark walnut from her bag and cracked it against the kitchen table before holding it up and blowing its contents carefully over Cinderella. Black dust that tasted of coal glittered around her and she was sure she heard the echo of men singing as metal clanged against rocks, and then butterflies tumbled from Cinderella's stomach and tingles like tiny wings flooded through her limbs leaving her breathless. For a moment she was in a whirlwind of sparkling stars. Her skin trembled as cold air touched her and then she gasped as some thing tugged hard at her waist and back; stays being tightened.

Finally, she looked down. Her dowdy house dress was gone. Now she wore a fine silver gown, pinched at the waist and sleeveless. Diamonds shone here and there in the silk and her skin glittered as if the stars that had spun around her head had settled there. She turned to look in the small mirror on the kitchen wall and almost didn't recognise herself. Her curls were styled half-up and half-down, and more jewels shone from within the deep red. Her face was painted and her lips glistened pink.

'It's magic,' she breathed, finally.

'All beauty is magical. You'll learn that,' the fairy godmother said softly. 'But it's not a magic you can control.'

'I do look beautiful though,' Cinderella said, smiling. 'The prince will surely fall in love with me.'

'Oh, you little fool.' The fairy godmother laughed, and it was like the sound of ice splintering. 'They will *all* be beautiful. It's the Prince's Bride Ball, after all. It will take more than a pretty face and a smart dress to snare him. Thankfully, you have those slippers on your feet.' Cinderella looked down. They were the most beautiful shoes she'd ever seen.

'Are they glass?'

'Don't be so ridiculous. Do you want to walk on glass? They're diamond.' She turned them this way and that so the light caught and reflected every sparkle of silver in Cinderella's dress from their surfaces. 'Diamond and something entirely of their own, too. They're charmed.' She looked at Cinderella, her clear blue eyes cold and calculating. 'They'll make you charming.'

'They fit perfectly.' The shoes were lighter than she expected and warm.

'I imagine they fit when they want to,' the fairy godmother purred.

Cinderella smiled. The high heels made her taller than the strange exquisite woman in her kitchen. She felt elegant. They were perfect. They were also soft and warm against the soles of her feet. They were shoes she could dance all night in.

'Here is a second nut,' the fairy godmother said, hiding the dark shelled magic behind some plates on the second shelf of the dresser. 'Crack it as I did and inhale the dust tomorrow night and you will be transformed again.' The fairy godmother clapped her hands together. 'And now you're ready.'

'I can't believe you're doing this for me,' Cinderella was almost bursting with excitement. 'Thank you so much. You've made my dreams come true.' With a rush of warmth she tried to hug the fairy godmother, but instead of embracing her, the icy woman gripped her arms tightly, breaking off the gesture before it had begun. She didn't let go.

'I didn't say it wasn't without a price.'

'What do you mean?' The slim fingers were digging into her skin so tightly she was afraid they'd leave bruises.

'Nothing comes without a price.' Slowly the fairy

godmother released her. 'I can do this for you, but there is something I need in return.'

Cinderella remained silent and listened. Whatever it was, she knew she'd do it. To have her wish taken from her now would break her heart.

'You will get your precious prince should you so want him. When he invites you to live in the castle with him in preparation for your glorious wedding, I want you to explore every room there. A servant of mine, the same one who is waiting outside with your carriage to take you there, will come to you every night and you will report your findings to him.'

'Every room? But there must be hundreds.'

'Castles are never quite as big as they seem from the outside.' Her eyes darkened and for a moment Cinderella thought her fairy godmother looked sad and wounded rolled into one. 'From the inside they can be quite claustrophobic,' she finished softly, lost in a world that Cinderella couldn't penetrate.

'Every room, though. You understand?

Cinderella nodded. 'I understand.'

The fairy godmother studied her for a moment, before pulling a third walnut from the bodice of her dress. Unlike the others, the shell was so dark it was almost black and it was small and gnarled, as if dug up fossilised from the forest earth. 'This one,' she said softly, 'you break in case of emergency. But only after you've searched the castle.'

'What kind of emergency?' Cinderella asked.

'If castle life doesn't turn out quite as you planned. If you need a quiet escape.'

Cinderella thought of the castle and the handsome prince. 'I doubt I'll need that,' she said, defiantly.

'Good.' The fairy godmother smiled and stood up, picking up her bag. 'And now you shall go to the ball.' She snapped her fingers and the back door opened.

A fine silver carriage was waiting on the street. Two grey ponies with impossibly black manes pranced eagerly in the reins. A rugged man jumped down from the seat and held the delicate door open. Even in the dark, Cinderella could see that the seats were made of red velvet and lined with gold trim. The driver's hand was strong as he took hers and helped her step up. She muttered a thank you, but all her attention was on the glory of her dress and her carriage and the thought of the prince.

'Don't forget our arrangement.' Her fairy godmother stood on the pavement watching her through the open door. 'It won't go well for you if you forget.'

'I won't forget.' Cinderella heard the menace in the woman's words and shivered slightly. 'And thank you.'

'One more thing,' the fairy godmother pushed the door closed. 'Make sure you leave by midnight at the very latest. Both nights.'

'Midnight?' Inside the carriage, Cinderella's smile fell.

'But the last dances will barely have started by then. He'll dance with others. He'll forget me.'

'You have a lot to learn about men. Wind him up then leave him wanting.' She smiled but there was a touch of bitterness in it. 'That's where your real power lies.' She nodded to the driver. 'Midnight. Don't forget!'

And then the carriage was moving under her. When Cinderella peered out to the street behind them, the fairy godmother was gone. There were just the faint fireflies of sparkles left in the cold, night air.

The temperature was dropping as night took hold, but Cinderella hardly noticed the chill as she stepped down at the entrance to the castle. She could barely breathe with the beauty of it. No wonder her step-mother was so keen to get back into favour at court if it meant visiting here often. She wondered how she could have borne losing it in the first place. Built entirely from white marble, the castle rose up in elegant towers that surrounded the main building, each a different height from the rest, and each with a burning beacon at its tip.

The tales told that in the days of dragons the great beasts would sweep and circle the lights of the castle in their mating rituals before flying to the far mountain to nest. She could believe it. They looked like stars hanging low and smiling down on her sudden good fortune. Tonight it looked as if there were candles burning in every window of every tower for the ball. She ached at the sight of it.

'At the end of the day, it's just a house.'

Cinderella realised that, lost in her awe of the castle, she hadn't let go of the driver's hand after he'd helped her down. She quickly pulled it away.

'It's beautiful,' she said.

'Beauty can be overrated.' His dark eyes seemed to be mocking her. 'And it fades.'

Her skin flushed slightly. 'Well, it will be my beauty that captures the prince,' she said, defiant. 'Wait and see.'

He laughed, his weathered face cracking into a grin, and she was surprised at what a warm sound it was.

'What's so funny?' she asked. He unsettled her. She didn't like it.

'That you think you're the hunter this evening.' He bowed slightly. 'Now run along inside and prance with all the other pretty little deer and let your shoes do their work. Just be back here by midnight. I'll be waiting.'

She lifted her chin and glared at him, before turning and making her way up the elegant stairs to the footmen waiting at the door. She didn't look back. He could laugh at her all he wanted, she didn't care. He was nobody. Nothing. Who cared what he thought?

By the time she came down the red-carpeted stairs into the main ballroom, all thoughts of the rude driver were gone from her head. At one side a champagne fountain flowed over a tower of delicate glasses. Footmen were spaced out at intervals along the walls, their wigs dusted blue to match their jackets. Music played, an elegant waltz, and beyond the sea of young women and the prince's noble friends, she could see the masked band, all dressed in white and raised high on a glass stage. It was everything she'd imagined and more. She took a glass of champagne from a passing waiter and was surprised by how steady her hand was. She'd expected to be more nervous, but with the warmth tingling through her from her shoes she breezed into the room, her head held high. She would be confident and mysterious, just like her fairy godmother.

She sipped her drink, enjoying the bubbles but not so keen on the sharp taste, and scanned the room. It was a sea of colour, each of the noble women in the city wearing the finest dresses their money could afford. Her own silver dress nearly faded in comparison, but as she walked further into the vast ball room heads turned her way as she passed, and voices dropped to a hush. The women eyed her suspiciously, but the men's glances ran the length of her body and lingered. She fought the urge to smile. She would be the belle of the ball. She really, really would. She didn't return any of the young men's smiles. There was only one man she was interested in dancing with; the prince himself.

When he came into view she stopped short and drew in a

breath, her heart suddenly racing. He was the most handsome man she'd ever seen. She'd wondered if he could match the picture she kept by her bed, but now she knew that was really just a poor imitation. He was tall and broad, and was dressed all in black. His dirty blond hair was smoothly combed to one side, and his perfect face was tanned. Cinderella watched, entranced, as he danced with a short girl in a blue dress. He moved effortlessly and the girl was obviously already in love with him, but it was also obvious that however charming the prince was, he wasn't focusing much of his attention on his partner. His smile was going over her shoulder to someone just out of Cinderella's sight.

'He's still looking at her.'

'Why her? He's danced with her twice. She's the only one he's danced with twice. I mean, she's not even that pretty.'

'She's interesting looking though.'

'If you like that sort of thing.'

Cinderella wasn't sure which of the gathered girls around her was whispering and she didn't look, but she did listen hard. Someone had already seized the prince's attention? Her stomach twisted in a cold sickly knot. Who? Who was her competition? Her feet burned in her shoes.

'And you know what her mother did, don't you? She left an Earl for a secretary! How ridiculous! Maybe he just feels sorry for her.'

Cinderella leaned on a pillar to steady herself. Rose?

They were talking about Rose? Surely they couldn't be? She stepped forward, suddenly having to know. It didn't take more than a moment to spot Rose standing at the edge of the circle watching the prince dance, her red dress matching the flush high in her cheeks. She was smiling at the prince and her face was transformed into something very close to beautiful. The weight she'd lost in the diet she'd been forced to undertake had made her features stronger, and for the first time Cinderella realised that her step-sister wasn't ugly at all. Unusual perhaps, but not ugly. She gritted her teeth. She wouldn't lose her prince to Rose. Not to Rose of all girls.

The music stopped and a smattering of applause ran round the room. Many of the girls were now turning their attention to the other noblemen in the room, realising that the prince's eye had already been taken but there were plenty of other good matches to be made at this Royal Bride Ball. Cinderella looked down at her shoes. They twinkled reflected silver from her dress, like moonlight on water. She took a deep breath. This was magic. And Rose couldn't fight magic.

The prince, after bowing politely to the girl who was no doubt already forgotten in his mind, but who would probably remember the feel of his hand on her back for the rest of her life, was heading back towards Rose.

Cinderella made her move. With her back to her step-sister, she crossed the room, cutting into the prince's path.

Her arm brushed his and she looked up at him, her eyes wide. 'I'm so sorry, your highness.' She dropped into a curtsey. 'I should have looked where I was going.'

'No, I should have looked...' his eyes had been locked on Rose, but now he glanced down at Cinderella. It was enough. The end of the sentence drained away. He held his hand out to her. 'I don't believe we've danced this evening. I would have remembered.'

'We haven't.'

'Then we should rectify that.' Without taking his eyes from hers, he pulled her close, much closer than he'd danced with the last girl. His arm was strong around her waist, and every inch of her skin tingled at his touch. Her face was inches from his neck and she could smell his scented warmth. She looked up at him and their lips almost brushed.

'Who are you?' he whispered.

'I'm...' She thought of Rose and her step-mother somewhere close by and she thought of her father, the secretary, and in the end she said all she could think of to escape discovery. 'Names can wait until later. Just dance with me.'

'As you wish, mystery girl,' he said and when he smiled she thought that all the beauty in the world was caught up in that expression. She melted into his embrace and let him whirl her around the floor, their feet in perfect harmony against the marble. She didn't care if Rose or her step-mother saw her. She didn't even look for them. As far as Cinderella was concerned no one else existed. It was just her, her handsome prince and the music. She had no concept of time passing; she was simply caught up in a moment she wanted to last forever. Eventually, the musicians paused for a rest, and the prince led Cinderella to a seat at the side of the room, the two of them sharing a velvet bench, his courtiers ensuring the rest of the guests allowed them some privacy. Cinderella still turned her head sideways and tilted her face down in case her step-mother or Rose should stare at her too hard.

'I've dreamed of meeting you,' she said, the words blurting out before she could stop them. She blushed slightly. 'I know that sounds stupid.'

'It's uncanny,' the prince murmured. 'I feel as if I know you and I don't even know your name. From the moment I saw you, my heart, well...' He leaned forward and touched her hand. 'Everyone else faded... I just *knew*.'

His hand was warm against hers and as he stroked the back of her hand gently with his thumb, she could feel her breath getting quicker. His face was thoughtful as his eyes searched hers.

'I'd given up on love, you know. True love.' He had leaned in closer to her and their lips were almost touching as they spoke. Cinderella longed to touch his face, to feel his hands on her. Her heart thumped in her chest. This was everything she'd dreamed of since she'd been a little girl. She'd never seen such a beautiful man, and here he was, and he wanted her.

'So much isn't as it seems, don't you think?' he said. 'But this, it's magical.'

'Love at first sight,' she said. She ignored the faintly unsettled feeling the mention of magic gave her.

'Yes,' he said. 'I do believe it is.'

'Shall we dance again?' she said. She wanted to feel his body against hers and wrap her arms around his neck and move freely. Break away from the formality of the set pieces. More than anything, she wanted to kiss him.

'Your wish is my command,' he said.

She felt as if she was floating when she got to her feet, and it was only when she glanced at the clock as they passed it, that she came crashing back to earth. It was quarter past eleven. It couldn't be. Her heart raced. Leave by midnight or be home by midnight? What had the fairy godmother said? She couldn't take the chance of being late. Of having the second night stolen from her. The night when the prince would *choose*.

'Would you excuse me for a moment?' she looked up at him, and let her eyes absorb the perfection of his face, storing it in memory. 'I must...' she wasn't quite sure how to finish the sentence. Thankfully, he simply nodded.

'Hurry back, my love.'

She tore herself away before she lost her determination, and then scurried through the revellers towards the stairs. She didn't look back.

* * *

The carriage was waiting for her, the driver leaning against the door watching as she fled the castle.

'Did you meet your handsome prince?' he asked. Again, there was a tone in his gruff voice that hinted he was laughing at her. She glared at him, wanting him to move away from the door so she could climb in. Although broad, he wasn't as tall as the prince, and where her love was blond and beautiful, this man had dark hair that hung slightly over his eyes and rough stubble peppered his chin and cheeks. His brown eyes made her nervous. She couldn't read them.

'Yes I did,' she said. 'Now get me back home before we're both in trouble.'

He laughed a little, an earthy sound, and stepped back, pulling the door with him and giving a brief mock bow as she climbed in.

'I was born in trouble it seems,' he said. 'But at least I'm no pansy prince who can't take care of himself.'

'What do you mean?' Cinderella asked, leaning forward in her seat. He either didn't hear her or just refused to answer because suddenly the wheels were turning and they were on their way. He was jealous, she decided. Who wouldn't be? The prince had everything a woman could want. That much was obvious. And he was going to be hers. That thought made her smile and, as they raced back to the house, she lost herself in the memory of his touch on her hand and the way he'd held her close as they danced.

* * *

The magic vanished as soon as she'd stepped through the kitchen door, her hair tumbling free down her shoulders and her fine silver gown evaporating to leave her back in her house dress. Her feet cooled as her own shoes, clunky and uncomfortable in comparison, replaced the diamond slippers. She was still smiling though, and made sure the other two nuts were safely into her pocket before drinking a glass of her father's wine and dancing with a broomstick across the kitchen floor and giggling to herself.

She'd barely crept upstairs in the dark and crawled into her cold bed by the time the front door slammed and lights went on throughout the house. She could hear her step-mother shouting. She was sure Rose was crying.

'You stupid, stupid girl!'

'It wasn't my fault, I—'

'You *had* him. In the palm of your hand! All my dreams – all your dreams – shattered!'

'Look, mother, I did my best—'

'Well it wasn't good enough!'

Cinderella pulled her knees up under her chin. Her excitement and the glow of love still burned in the pit of her stomach, but hearing her step-mother screeching so hysterically was something new and it gave her a sickening twist. As did Rose's sobbing.

'I'm sorry. I'm sorry—'

'Sorry isn't good enough! You're ruined everything! Everything!'

Cinderella pulled the covers over her head and pushed her fists into her ears. She wouldn't let them spoil her happiness. She wouldn't. And if she did win the prince's hand the next night then she made a quiet promise to herself that she'd find an Earl for Rose to marry. A handsome one.

The next day passed interminably, and once her chores were done she hid in her room avoiding her step-mother. She veered from berating Rose to encouraging her to make the best of the second night to come while Cinderella wished the hours away. Finally, night came round again and she watched from the window as Rose went off in Ivy's carriage. This time, however, she felt no jealousy, just her own overwhelming excitement. Once her father had gone up to his study to work into the early hours, she ran down to the kitchen and cracked the second nut open.

This time, her dress shone like spun gold, reflecting every shade of red from her magnificent hair. Her feet tingled with the warmth from the slippers and her face glowed.

'Very nice,' the driver said, as he opened the door, 'if you like that kind of thing.'

'Are you being rude to me on purpose?' Cinderella asked, frowning at him. 'If you think I'm so ugly just keep your opinions to yourself.'

He smiled again, laughing at her she was sure. 'What?' she snapped, crossly.

'It wasn't the raw product I was commenting on, it was all the trimmings. You look like a proper little court lady, that's for sure.'

'What's so wrong with that? That's what I *want* to be.'

'Nothing. It suits some. I just prefer a real woman, that's all. The type who runs free through the forest. Now, let's get you to your perfect prince, shall we?'

She didn't say another word, but pressed her lips tightly together. She could quite happily not speak to the insufferable brute for the rest of her life.

Rose was trying to talk to the prince as Cinderella swept into the ballroom, and she was glad to see that he was showing no interest in her whatsoever. If anything, he looked distracted and irritated, his glance going this way and that, scanning the room. Her heart lifted at the sight of him and she took a glass of champagne and waited until he'd fully spurned her step-sister, sending her scurrying to the sides of the ballroom in shame, before she approached him.

'Hello,' she said, simply, as his mouth dropped open.

'You! You're here! You look...' He stared at her and smiled. 'Perfect.'

'I'm sorry I left,' she said, as he took her in his arms and swept her onto the dance floor. Around them, couples pulled back slightly and the partnerless young women drifted into the corners to console each other. It was clear the prince had eyes for no other. He had come back to life with her arrival, his listlessness suddenly shed like a second skin.

'I thought you had left me,' he said. 'I couldn't sleep. I've thought of nothing but you.'

'I've been the same,' she said and smiled. Could he have become more handsome overnight? It seemed that way. Once again, just like the previous night, they danced and talked and revelled in each other's presence until he gave a signal and the music paused, and then the prince took her hand and led Cinderella out towards the balcony.

'Let's go somewhere more private,' he whispered into her ear. His voice was like electricity running through her, and she simply nodded. She was breathless. Her skin was flushed. Two servants pulled the glass doors open for them and they stepped out into the night. The doors closed, sealing them off from the rest of the party. No one would join them out here, that was clear, and now that the dance had stopped Cinderella was glad to be away from the rest of the guests. Rose and her step-mother wouldn't be expecting to see her here, and certainly not dressed so glamorously, but that still wouldn't stop them recognising her if they looked for too long – and every one's eyes had been on her by the time the music finished. Everyone thought the prince had made his choice.

At some point while they'd danced soft snowflakes had started to fall, but the balcony was covered in a silk canopy and fires burned in ornate metal stands and the air was warm. Cinderella was sure that even if it was pouring with icy rain she wouldn't notice. Ahead of them the city was spread out, an ocean of darkness with only occasional ships of light in the gloom. It was late, and while the castle was still filled with music and dancing, the ordinary people had long days ahead. As she stood at the low wall that ran around the balcony, looking out over it all, she felt a lifetime away from the grime and cold of the city's winter.

She looked up at the handsome man beside her and smiled. The prince, saying nothing, pulled her close, one arm wrapping tight around her. He lifted his other hand and traced his fingers down her face and to her neck, his eyes lingering on her skin. Her breath came more rapidly as her stomach knotted with longing. Each controlled touch sent a thousand shivers through her. His hand finally reached the curve of her breasts, which pushed upwards as the dress was designed to have them do, and she arched her back against him slightly, unable to control herself. She moaned softly as he brushed over her skin and then he lifted his gaze and his eyes met hers. He leaned forward and finally they kissed.

His mouth was warm and soft, and his lips were gentle, barely touching hers at first and then pressing harder as she responded, his hands exploring her body through the confines of her dress. She touched him back, her fingers running down his chest, and then resting one hand on his thigh, his leg strong beneath the material of his trousers. Unable to stop herself, she lifted the hand higher, enjoying the heat coming from him, and the urgency of his breath. He kissed her harder, his hand pulling at her skirts and she thought of Buttons' fingers, slim and feminine and wondered how different the prince's would feel.

She barely heard the clock chimes ringing out. She was lost in the moment, fireworks exploding in her mind and sending traces of intensity throughout her body. Even in her fantasies it had never been like this. She wanted to pull his clothes free and feel his skin next to hers. She couldn't stand the longing, she was desperate for him. His hands were struggling with her underskirts and she wanted to tug them up and give him access. All childish thoughts fell away from her and she was suddenly all woman, eager to do all the things she had only heard about from Ivy and from the other, less well-behaved, girls in the town.

'It's only midnight,' he said, as the first chime echoed across the city. 'We have hours yet. We could go somewhere and—'

'Midnight?' Her head still a haze, Cinderella could barely focus, but the word cut through the heat that filled her. 'It's midnight?'

'Yes, but—'

She broke free from him so suddenly it took him by surprise. His arms fell away, and by the time he reached for her again she was already at the doors. She had to leave by midnight, even though every inch of her wanted to stay in the prince's arms and kiss him all night. The fairy godmother's icy expression flashed behind her eyes. She had to do as she'd been told.

'I have to leave!' she called back as she yanked the door open, grasping the handle from the footman in order to get back in more quickly. 'I'm sorry. I have to leave.'

She let her eyes drink in his handsome face one more time and then she turned and fled. As she pushed her way through the dancing couples, she knew he was coming after her. She kept ahead and finally broke clear of the ballroom, running down the sweeping red staircase to the exit. She could see the carriage, door open, waiting for her, the rough driver already sitting at the reins.

'Hurry up!' he called.

'Wait!' the prince shouted, chasing her down the stairs. 'Wait! I don't even know your name!'

Cinderella ran faster still and threw herself, all dignity forgotten, into the back of the carriage that was already beginning to move away. She dragged the door closed as the horses picked up speed, and then, recovering her breath, she peered back through the window. The prince was staring after her, one hand reaching out as if he could somehow pull the carriage back to him. The cold night air gripped one foot and she looked down and the last chime rang out. One of her enchanted shoes was missing. How could it have come off? And when? They fitted so perfectly. And what would her fairy godmother say?

As it turned out, the fairy godmother was waiting for them and as Cinderella climbed out of the coach in her dull house dress with her hair loose, she didn't seem overly concerned about the diamond slipper. 'It'll find its way back, I'm sure,' she said and smiled as if she understood something that Cinderella didn't. That didn't surprise Cinderella. She thought there were probably a lot of things the fairy godmother understood that were beyond her own reach.

The night was cold and she was suddenly tired, even though her heart was racing.

'You've got your prince. Now remember your promise,' the fairy godmother said. 'Do what I asked of you or none of this will end well.'

Cinderella nodded. Not that she knew how she was ever going to get back into the castle again. The prince didn't even know her name, and she'd been in too much of a panic to shout it to him.

'And you,' the fairy godmother glanced at the driver as a flurry of stardust swallowed up both her and the glittering coach, 'Remember, it'll be morning soon.' By the time she'd finished the sentence, the echo of the words were all that was left of her. Cinderella shivered and glared at him. 'You were going to drive away without me.'

'I knew you'd make it.' He leaned on the wall. 'Did you get what you wanted? Is true love in the air?'

'What would you know about it?'

'I know a few things,' he said, leaning in closer, one hand teasing a strand of her wild red hair. Cinderella pressed herself back against the kitchen door, but she could feel his musky heat and she still throbbed from her embrace with the prince. He touched her hair. She couldn't help but shiver slightly and she couldn't decide if it was revulsion or attraction.

'I know your hair looks prettier free than trapped,' he said. 'Like most things. I also know princes are just men. Mainly not very good ones. And a castle can't give a girl like you what the woman inside will want.'

'You don't know anything.' Why did he make her feel so uncomfortable and awkward? Why couldn't he just shut up and leave?

'I know you're no court lady.' He smiled, his teeth white

and even against his rugged face. 'And it would be a shame to see you turn into one.'

'The prince loves me,' she said, defiantly.

'So you say. But do you love him?'

Finally, behind her back, she found the latch to the gate and pushed it open. 'That's none of your business.' He was so arrogant. Who was he anyway? Just some lackey. She stomped down the stairs to the kitchen door. 'But yes,' she said. 'I think I do!' She closed the door behind her without looking back.

5

'Help me...'

Over the course of the two days after the prince's last Bride Ball a black storm raged over the city. A fierce wind blew down from the mountain so hard that they said it was the ghostly fire of the dead dragons' breath, so long cold in their graves. It blew the snow canopy from the forest into the city streets. Thunder and lightning waged a war in clouds so low that those brave enough to venture out claimed that if they stretched an arm up they could touch them. The sky was a roiling ocean and all the people could do was to huddle round their small fires and wait for it to pass.

The anger of the storm outside, however, was nothing compared to the dark atmosphere that gripped Cinderella's house. Ivy, like everyone else in the city who had heard of the strange turn of events at the second ball, braved the weather and visited her sister and mother. She didn't stay long. Cinderella hid while her step-mother railed at Ivy for not helping them more, and then launched into a bitter attack on the pathetic physicality of her noble husband. Ivy slapped her and left. The house stood in silence for a long time after that, the girls staying in their rooms to avoid being caught by a wandering lash of Esme's tongue.

Rose got everything worst. Her pale skin was constantly blotched from crying and, at every meal time, Cinderella and her father would listen to the digs and jibes and feel the stings with her. Esme was drinking too. It was as if something inside her had cracked. Finally, as she berated Rose once more for being useless and destroying all her dreams of her old life which she'd come so close to achieving, Cinderella's father finally slammed his hand down on the table and stood up.

'If this life is so bloody terrible, Esme, why did you choose it? It was love that mattered then? Don't you love me now?'

Cinderella and Rose both shrank down in their chairs. Their parents didn't argue. They didn't appear to have much in common, but they never fought.

'Don't be so ridiculous,' Wine spilled from her glass as Esme looked up. 'This isn't about love, this is about life! Ever since Ivy married that idiot Viscount—'

'He's not an idiot. If you took time to talk to him—'

'He's an idiot. He doesn't even go to court. But having been back to the castle and remembered what my life used to be like—'

'You hated it. You said it was shallow. You ran away from it, Esme, don't you remember? You were married to a man you loathed because of that life? You slept with that randy old bastard for five long years, every night of which you hated. That's what that life gave you!'

The two young women were forgotten in the heat of the fight, but Cinderella wished she could just slide down to the floor and crawl away. Worse still was the thought that this was all her fault. She still clung to her bubble of joy over her time at the castle but she'd been so focused on chasing what she'd wanted she hadn't considered the fallout.

'Yes, but if Rose had married the prince then I could have had the best of that life *and* you. I'm tired of all those people sniggering at us – at *me*. I'm tired of being poor. I'm tired of being cold. Don't you understand it?'

'I understand that. And I'm trying hard. But you can't have everything in life, it doesn't work that way. You have to decide what the important parts are.' The fight went out of Cinderella's father. 'The thing I don't understand anymore is you.' He turned his back on them and left the room. No one spoke after that.

In the morning, Rose and Cinderella cleared away the breakfast things and were doing the washing up, the two working slowly together in the relative safety of the basement room.

'Don't you have to take care of your hands?' Cinderella asked, as Rose scrubbed at a roasting tin. The other girl let out a short bitter bark of laughter.

'I don't think the softness of my skin matters any more. Not to mother, anyway.'

'There'll be other balls.' Cinderella felt a surprising wave of affection for her step-sister. Rose had always been the practical one. The clever one. Rose did not cry or get over emotional. Not even when they'd been children.

'You don't get it, Cinderella.' Rose sighed, tired. 'You never do. If the prince had just danced with me once, like the other girls, or not even danced with me at all, then that would have been okay. But I'm now the girl who wasn't good enough. I'm the *discarded* one.' She put the dish down and leaned on the side of the sink as if she didn't have the energy to stand. 'Even after that other girl ran off the prince didn't want anything to do with me. Mother made me try and talk to him and he brushed me off. In front of *everyone*, as if I suddenly disgusted him.'

Tears, always so close, welled up in her eyes. 'Now none of the other noblemen will come near me. I've made everything worse. All that effort mother put in to get me ready for the ball and it's come to nothing.' She sniffed hard. 'She's going through the change and I think this on top of that has driven her a bit mad. I think she's driving me mad.'

Cinderella's eyes fell away from her step-sister's. She had been so happy that night. She and the prince were meant to be, she was sure of it. Whenever she closed the door of her room and looked at his picture, she was transported back to the wonders of the ball, and his arms around her and his kiss... and she fantasised about him finding her and all being as her fairy godmother promised and life being wonderful. But every time she looked at Rose or her step-mother she felt bad. She wondered if maybe she should tell Rose what happened? How the other girl was her? Maybe Rose would actually be relieved, be cause then they could send for the prince and her step-mother would have the life she wanted and it would all be well again.

'Look, Rose—' she started, and then the back door opened and a burst of fresh cold and rain delivered Buttons into the kitchen.

'Evening, princess,' he said. 'Sorry I didn't knock. It's a bastard out there.' He pushed the door closed and then hurried over to the stove – handing Rose the small sack he carried before pressing his palms against the warm metal and shivering. 'You must be Rose,' he grinned. 'I've heard about you.'

Rose looked in the bag and then pulled out a large round of cheese, a ham and two loaves of bread. 'And you must be the boy who's been refilling our coal scuttle when it empties,' she said wryly.

'That could be me, I confess.'

Cinderella couldn't look at Rose. She'd thought no one had noticed the gifts Buttons had been bringing her, but clearly that wasn't the case. 'Thanks, Buttons.'

'No problem, princess.'

Rose visibly flinched at the use of the word, but she pulled a chair up for him and poured him a hot coffee from the pot. 'You shouldn't be out on the streets in this if you don't have to be,' she said. 'Aside from the trouble you could get into. I'm presuming you didn't buy this stuff.'

'Can't keep me from the ladies,' He winked at her and then smiled at Cinderella. 'And it won't be missed. They have plenty.' He sat down. 'Anyway, I thought you'd want all the latest gossip from the castle, princess. You never get tired of that.'

'If it's about the Bride Balls, don't bother,' Rose said, bristling slightly. 'We know all about it.'

'But do you know about the shoe?' Buttons asked. Cinderella's heart leapt and Rose frowned.

'What shoe?'

'The one the girl left behind. They found it on the stairs when the party was being cleaned up. It's beautiful apparently. Made of diamonds or something. A dainty, narrow slipper that the prince is convinced belongs to his mystery beauty. He's totally all over the place. Quite funny to see. He was moping about like a teenager until they found it.'

'Really?' Cinderella fought back her smile although inside she was dancing all over again. He loved her! He felt the same way she did.

'Anyway,' Buttons continued. 'He's sending his footman on a tour of the city to try the slipper on the foot of every girl of the right age. When the slipper finds its owner, he'll marry her.'

'But that's ridiculous! It's a shoe. It'll fit a lot of girls,' Rose said. 'Surely you just look for the girl who has the other shoe.'

'I've seen it,' Buttons said. 'There's something funny about that slipper. And our handsome highness wants the girl who can wear it perfectly.'

'When does the search start?' Cinderella tried to keep the excitement out of her voice, but she wanted to sing with happiness. The slipper wouldn't fit anyone else, no matter how logical Rose's point was. It would be too big or too small for every lady but her. It would make itself that way. Her stomach fizzed. The fairy godmother's promise was going to come true.

'Tomorrow. But even if they work all day and night it's still going to take weeks to go through the whole city.'

'Not necessarily,' Rose said. 'Maybe they'll find her quickly.' There was a longing in her voice and then she sighed. She looked up at Cinderella, her face full of despair. 'If we could keep this from mother, that would be good.'

Cinderella nodded. The mood dampened after that, and Buttons, now warm and dry got up to leave. Rose gave him an extra scarf to wrap tight around his face against the outside onslaught and both girls waved him off.

A small brown mouse ran in between their legs and sat shivering on the floor, half under the stove. Rose reached for the broom to shoo it out, but Cinderella stopped her. 'The little thing will die out in that weather. Leave it be. I think it's rather sweet.' She then broke a small chunk of the cheese off and dropped it on the floor. 'Now come on, let's go upstairs. We can't hide in here forever.'

Cinderella's step-mother had heard about the slipper by lunchtime. Everybody had. In a city that was besieged by bad weather it seemed gossip could still travel faster than the icy wind. A fevered light came on in her eyes as she gathered all the information she could about the shoe, paying money they didn't have to the servants of those whose houses had already been visited for every tiny detail. She clapped her hands together and smiled and laughed. There was still a chance for Rose – there was still a chance for *her*.

'But it's not my shoe,' Rose said. 'And he doesn't want me.' It was a plaintive, quiet protest of one who knows they're already defeated.

'He wants whoever that shoe fits,' Esme countered. 'If it fits you, he'll marry you.'

She spent a lot of time examining Rose's feet. They were too wide for the slipper, she decided, and so she bound them so tightly in bandages that the poor girl could barely walk without crying. Cinderella's father tried to stop it, but Rose said it was fine and that it didn't hurt that much and she just wanted to make her mother happy. Every morning and every night the bandages would come off and Esme would force her poor daughter to try to squeeze her bruised foot into a shoe which was purportedly the exact size of the sparkling one that was stopping at each house in the city. It should be – Cinderella's step-mother had paid enough for it.

Rose's foot never fit. It wasn't the length that was the problem, it was the width. Rose might have lost weight but her feet were still wide. After five days of binding, Cinderella's step-mother decided more drastic action was needed. She plunged her daughter's bare feet into buckets of ice for hours at a time and then bandaged them up again.

Cinderella wasn't sure what was the most disturbing – her actions or the soothing way she spoke to Rose as she did them. She loved her, she said. She just wanted the best for her, she said. And all the time Rose cried and the storm outside continued to rage. Cinderella just wished the prince's procession would hurry up and get to them. This madness needed to stop.

The night before it happened, the storm finally broke. The skies cleared and the wind dropped, leaving the city in an icy calm.

Rose finally broke too.

Upstairs on the top floor two middle-aged people, once brought together by true love, now shouted and sobbed at each other. Cinderella heard the words, 'menopause' and 'hormones' and then her step-mother completely lost it, attacking her husband with a barrage of insults whose targets ranged from his manhood to his wages. Cinderella had been keeping mainly to her room. No one was paying her any attention anyway, and once she'd done her chores for the day she'd go and lock herself away with her lover's picture, close her eyes and turn time back to the night of the ball. This time even that daydream couldn't block out the fighting. It was gone ten at night when she crept into the kitchen and found Rose.

At first she couldn't quite take it in. The bandages were undone and spread all over the floor. Rose, her hair free around her shoulders, was sitting on a wooden chair, one knee tucked under her chin. She was sobbing and muttering incoherently, focused intently on whatever she was trying to do. Cinderella's eyes widened. What *was* she trying to do?

Rose had gripped her little toe with one hand, separating it from the rest, and was cutting at it with a small knife. She paused, and with a bloody hand reached for the bottle of brandy on the kitchen table and took a long swallow from it. Only when she put it back down did she see Cinderella. She stared for a moment.

'Help me,' she said eventually, her words thick through the snot and sweat that covered her face. 'I can't quite cut it off.' Tears came in a sudden rush, and the awful sobs broke Cinderella's shock. She ran to her, and grabbed the knife. Blood gushed, thick and red from the wound and her stomach lurched as she saw the protruding bone. She moved quickly, grabbing a bowl and running outside. She flew up to the street, fell to her hands and knees and filled it with icy snow. Her hands burned with the cold, but she didn't feel it. How could Rose do this? How could she have done this?

Back in the kitchen, she thrust her step-sister's foot into the bowl and held her as she shrieked with the pain. Then, while Rose drank more from the brandy bottle, Cinderella gently stitched her skin back up, coated it in medicinal salves and bandaged her two smallest toes together. She felt sick. Her family was crumbling into madness. And they were her family, she knew that in her heart, however much she sometimes felt separate from them.

'There you go,' she said, softly. 'That should heal.' Rose's foot would never be pretty to look at, but hopefully she'd keep her toe. She was tired. Rose was exhausted. What a mess it had all become. 'We should tell father,' she said. 'You probably need to see a doctor.' The floor was still slick with crimson and Cinderella reached for the mop.

Rose studied her, eyes glazed. 'Your mother didn't die, you know.' She sniffed and ran the back of her hand across her nose. 'You do know that, don't you?' Cinderella turned and the blood was forgotten as she leaned on the mop to keep herself standing. The world tilted slightly beneath her.

'What?'

'She didn't die,' Rose said, simply. 'She ran away with a travelling man. They were going to the Far Mountain to find the dragons. That's what she said.' She sighed. 'But she was a drunk. She said a lot of things, when she wasn't shouting at you or your father.'

'You're lying.' Unwanted images rose unbidden behind her eyes. Hiding behind bannisters. A woman laughing unpleasantly. Shouting.

'She used to come to my father's house and scream crazy things. She was wild, your mother. Wild and mean.'

'That's not true.'

'We didn't tell you because you were so little. We felt sorry for you.' Fresh tears filled her eyes. 'We loved you. You were like mine and Ivy's pretty little doll. My mother used to scoop you up and read you stories and stroke your hair until you slept. Why do you think you want to marry a prince so much? Who do you think told you those pretty stories of castle life?'

'No. No!' The walls of Cinderella's world crumbled, as Rose's words jarred with precious memories. 'That wasn't her! That was *my* mother. My dead mother.'

'We should have told you,' Rose was staring into space. 'We really should. Then maybe you wouldn't have grown up to be such a little bitch to us all the time.'

Cinderella turned and ran. She didn't look back.

6

'It finally fits!'

The sky was blue overhead and, although it remained freezing cold, the sun shone down on the street as the fanfare played and the procession of prince's men pulled up in their street. Cinderella's father refused to come downstairs. Even Esme was subdued as she and Rose waited in the sitting room, with Cinderella loitering in the back ground pretending to stoke up the fire. Rose, in her best dress, was sitting in an armchair. Her face was pale, no doubt she was in agony with her injured foot. Cinderella caught her eye and the two girls shared a wan smile. Esme didn't look at either of them. Cinderella wasn't sure she could bring herself to. The shouting had stopped when she'd seen what Rose had done, and there were dark circles around her eyes that no longer held fevered madness.

As the footmen swept in, the familiar diamond slipper glittering on a red cushion, for a brief moment Cinderella wished it would fit Rose so they could be done with it. Or better still, for it to fit neither of them and to pass them by.

'His royal highness has decreed that whomever this shoe fits, he shall take as his betrothed. Every young woman in the land is required to try it on.' The man looked tired and spoke the words wearily. 'Ma'am. If you would,' he said to Rose. He lowered the cushion and placed the shoe at her feet. Rose looked at it and laughed a little; a low sad sound. 'I cut the wrong foot,' she said, softly. 'How typical.'

'Ma'am?' the footman asked.

She ignored him and lifted her right foot, pushing it into the glass. Her heel hung half an inch over the back and she couldn't squeeze it in any further. Cinderella didn't think she tried very hard, and nor could she blame her.

'Well, that's that then,' Esme said. After all the hysteria of the previous two weeks, her voice was now calm and empty. 'Thank you.'

The footman picked up the shoe and brought it over to Cinderella, 'Ma'am. If you would.'

Cinderella's heart raced. She couldn't help it.

'She didn't go to the ball,' her step-mother said. 'You needn't bother with her.'

'All the ladies in the land.' The footman gave a small smile. In his exhaustion he could barely raise the corners of his mouth. 'Otherwise I'm going to have to start all over again.'

Cinderella carefully lifted her foot. She could feel the warmth from the strange diamond slipper already. Her sole had barely touched the inside when she felt it tighten gently around her, moulding itself to her shape.

There was a long moment's silence as the truth dawned on them all.

'It fits!' The footman's mouth had dropped open. 'It finally fits!'

'But that's not possible!' Esme was staring at her in disbelief. 'How did you... How... why didn't you say?'

'You.' Rose's voice was cold as she pulled herself upright painfully. 'It was you all along.'

It was Cinderella's turn to avoid their faces. Her heart raced with excitement but her stomach squirmed in shame. Still. She lifted her chin. She'd make it better for all of them. They'd see that when they calmed down. Surely they would.

There wasn't a lot of time for discussion. As soon the footman had stepped back outside with the shoe and announced that the girl had been found to the prince's guard, a team of men arrived to start packing up their possessions ready to move them into the castle and their new royal apartments. Whatever misgivings her step-mother might have initially had evaporated as the realisation that her dreams had been achieved after all took hold. She squeezed Cinderella's cheeks and kissed her on the forehead, declaring that she'd always been the prettiest of the girls and how could she not have recognised that glorious red hair when she'd seen it at the ball.

Cinderella had wanted to point out that it was probably because ever since Ivy got married Rose had been the sole focus of her attention, and she'd been pretty much forgotten, but decided that silence on the matter might be her best option. Esme took to directing the packers who were dismantling their old life and home with alarming speed. A little over an hour later several tailors showed up with a selection of fine dresses for the women and suits for Cinderella's father. Their old clothes would not do for life at the castle.

After they had fussed over Cinderella, dressing her in an ermine trimmed silver dress almost the same colour as the one she'd worn at the ball, she picked out several other dresses and took them upstairs. With her heart slightly in her mouth, she knocked on Rose's door. Her step-sister was sitting on the edge of her bed looking around at all her books and old toys that she'd never brought herself to throw away.

'I picked you out some dresses,' Cinderella said. 'They're very beautiful.'

Rose looked at her. 'Why didn't you just say?' She ignored the dresses and, feeling awkward, Cinderella lay them out across the mattress.

'They're all for you. I picked the prettiest ones.'

'You must have been laughing at me all this time.' Rose stared into space again. 'All this time.'

'No!' The words were like darts into Cinderella's heart. 'No, I wasn't! I just didn't know how to say... I didn't know what to say... I'm so sorry.' Tears stung her eyes.

'What did I ever do to you? You're my little sister. I've always looked after you.'

'Rose—I—'

'Just leave me alone. I'll put on one of your precious dresses. I wouldn't want to embarrass you in front of your prince.'

'I don't care about...' Cinderella couldn't finish the sentence. She *did* care about the prince. She cared that her family arrived looking as fine as they could. She cared about going to live in the castle and marrying the man all the girls wanted. She couldn't help it.

Rose smiled sadly. 'As long as you've got what you wanted, eh, Cinderella? I guess that's all that matters.'

Her face flushed, Cinderella backed out of the room and closed the door. A cold wind rushed up the stairs as men trekked in and out carrying clocks, chairs and boxes of china and cutlery that Esme deemed fit enough to take with them. Cinderella peered over the bannister. Her step-mother seemed to be taking a lot of their ordinary things. Why wouldn't she just leave them behind? There would be better things in the castle. Their possessions would just look cheap.

'I'm very disappointed in you.'

The voice made her jump, and she turned to see her father standing on the bottom step of the stairs that led up to his attic study. 'But now we're going to live in the castle,' she said. It sounded lame. It was. That wasn't what her father was talking about and she knew it.

'I can almost forgive the deception. Sneaking out to the ball – although how you did it I'll never know and I'm not sure I want to – was wrong, but I know how much you wanted to go. But this behaviour – watching everything your step-mother and Rose have been through these past few weeks—'

'She's been crazy!' Cinderella blurted out. 'That's not my fault.'

'Your step-mother is going through... well, there's a time of life that comes to all women. It's difficult. And times have been hard since the newspaper closed down and my work has been less regular. Your step-mother wants us to have both worlds. And if anyone can make that happen she can. We've talked about it. She thinks at court we could get the newspaper started again. We could make things better for a lot of people.' He paused and stared at Cinderella. 'But your behaviour towards your sister and the rest of us has been plain selfish. Perhaps it's our fault. We've always spoiled you. You were the favourite baby of the family.'

Spoilt? Her? Cinderella couldn't believe what she was hearing.

'I never thought I'd say this,' her father turned back to the stairs, 'but you're reminding me of your mother.'

Alone in the hallway, Cinderella's shock turned to anger and she seethed quietly. Where was the gratitude? She'd just completely changed their lives for the better! Where were the congratulations? She'd fallen in love and was going to marry the man of her dreams. Surely her own father should be happy for her? She stormed into her bedroom and slammed the door, and she didn't care if it made her sound like a child. Not even a spoilt one.

Her bad mood vanished once she stepped up into the golden carriage the prince sent for her, a silver one directly behind it for the rest of her family. The whole street came out to see them off, and Cinderella knew that at least her step-mother would be bursting with pride. Her respectability was being restored to her – in grand style – and it was all down to Cinderella. She settled back in the luxurious fur cushions and looked out of the window at all the ordinary people coming out of their houses, curious to see her as the delicate wheels carried her quickly back to the castle. It was a perfect distraction from thinking about the diamond slippers and the magic she had used to grab the prince's attention. He'd fall in love with her without them anyway. She was sure of that. He just had to get to know her.

He was waiting for her on the sweeping stairs, now coated in a red carpet, and lined with wigged courtiers. As she stepped down, the crowds who filled the streets and stretched out from their balconies to catch a glimpse of her, cheered wildly. Cinderella barely heard them. Although the rest of the city was still filthy after the storm the castle gleamed white and all the windows glinted in the winter sunshine truly making it a castle of light. It was as glorious in the daylight as it had been at night, and, Cinderella thought as she fell into a deep curtsey, so was the prince. She smiled at him and he smiled back, but there was an edge of wariness in the look. He snapped his fingers and a servant stepped forward quickly carrying the cushion with the shoe and placed it on the step in front of her.

Only when she slipped her foot into it again, lifting her leg elegantly so he could see how perfect the fit was, did the prince's smile break into a grin.

'My darling,' he said, leaning forward and kissing her. 'I'm so glad I've found you.' He looked up at the crowd. Around them the courtiers burst into cheers, and she took his arm as he led her into the castle.

Her family's apartments were quite magnificent. The living area alone was bigger than the ground floor of their old house, now locked up and forgotten, and windows ran almost from floor to ceiling, with heavy gold and silver drapes hanging to either side. Servants dashed here and there making lists of all their requirements, Esme insisting on having a writing desk and chair placed by the window with the best view of the city, where her husband could finish his novel and write his articles. Cinderella watched as her father smiled at her step-mother and she saw in that moment how much he loved her. He would not complain about this new life if it made her happy.

Rose's room was next to her own and there was an interconnecting door between the two vast boudoirs. Cinderella wondered if they'd ever use it. She doubted it. Not that she'd be in her own room for long. Soon they would have the wedding and she'd be in the prince's bed. She remembered how his kisses had made her feel on the night of the ball and wondered if she could wait until she was married. And would it matter that much if she didn't? The world was suddenly her oyster. Perhaps Rose wouldn't be in her room too long either. She'd be a fine catch for a nobleman now, and Cinderella was determined to advocate a good match for her, if only to ease the nagging sense of guilt she couldn't quite shake off.

The royal surgeon visited Rose that evening before dinner to examine her foot. Cinderella's new maids were dressing her when he left, but she was sure she could hear crying from the other room. Dismissing the two girls – and rather enjoying the powerful feeling that gave her – she opened the middle door a crack to hear what was being said.

'It's okay, mother,' Rose said. 'It's just a limp.'

'But needing a stick forever?' Esme was crying, one arm round her daughter. 'I'm so sorry. It was madness. It's all my fault.'

'Beauty has never been my finest feature. And *you* didn't try to cut my toe off. I did.'

'Because of me.'

'It's done now.' Rose kissed her mother's cheek. 'I love you. Now let's get ready for dinner and show the royal family we know how to play this game as well as they do.'

Cinderella closed the door and leaned against it, feeling slightly sick. How could her seizing her own happiness have caused so much unhappiness for others? It would get better. It would. She lay on her bed, careful not to mess up her freshly styled hair, and waited for dinner. She pushed all the sad thoughts from her mind and concentrated on how happy dancing with the prince had made her. She tried not to think about how the prince had been looking at Rose before she'd cut across his path that night, wearing her enchanted shoes. It made some thing in her stomach twist; something dark and unpleasant that made her feel like a thief.

The king was a large, gruff man whose hair was a shock of white beneath his crown and his formal robes were tight around a body that was once no doubt thick-set and muscular, but now was veering towards fat as the weight slipped from his chest and shoulders and settled around his middle. His eyes were still sharp though. When they'd been drinking champagne before dinner and the prince had introduced her, Cinderella had done her best to remember what she'd learned from eavesdropping on the lessons Rose had endured, and complimented him on his beautiful castle, and answered his questions as well as she could. But she couldn't help but be distracted by the hairs sprouting from his ears and nose and her knowledge of contemporary art and music was quite lacking.

They ate dinner without the queen, who was apparently indisposed with a chill, the delicate clinking of their silver knives and forks against the bone china echoing around the vast dining room. Cinderella sat opposite the prince, but it was Rose and Esme who sat to either side of the king himself, and Ivy and her Viscount made up the rest of the table, the group talking and leaving the young lovers with a little privacy to talk. Although the prince smiled at her often, their conversation was somewhat stilted, as if the passion they had felt two weeks previously had left them awkward in each other's company. Cinderella found herself reaching for her wine glass frequently to try and calm her nerves.

Rose, however, was having no trouble talking to the king.

'I think it's as many as fifteen children now,' she said. 'It's terrible. And they're all tradesmen's children because they can't afford to buy coal or logs from the merchants to warm their homes. So they have to go into the forest for firewood while their parents are working.'

'And no bodies are found? They're not simply being attacked by hungry wolves?'

'Who knows, your majesty. But I'm sure the people would feel much safer knowing you had soldiers in the woods protecting them.'

'Hmmm.' The king nodded.

'In fact,' Rose said, 'if your majesty's soldiers were to gather the firewood and give it to the children, it would be a sign of the great affection you obviously have for the ordinary people.' She sipped her wine. 'Such good feeling would probably make taxes easier to collect too.' The last sentence was spoken so delicately that it was almost an afterthought, but the king's heavily laden fork paused on its journey.

'I do love the people,' he said. 'This is true. And there are always spare soldiers.' He looked up at the prince. 'Did you know about these missing children?'

'I had heard something.' The prince shrugged, but it clearly wasn't a subject that interested him much. Cinderella thought of the baker's boy with his cheeky grin and she was proud of Rose for bringing it up.

'Why had I not heard about it?' The king frowned slightly. 'There used to be a newspaper. What happened to that?'

'It was closed down, your majesty,' Esme said. 'I believe

some of your advisors worried that copies would be smuggled out of the city to your enemies who would gain a greater understanding of your kingdom.'

'Advisors,' the king snorted. 'They do get over-enthusiastic.'

'My dear Henry was the editor,' Esme touched her husband's hand. 'I'm sure he could help re-start it should you so wish. There's really nothing like reading all the news from the streets' perspective before hearing it, from perhaps somewhat protective advisors.'

The king nodded. 'Perhaps you're right.' He looked at Esme and smiled. 'I remember your first wedding you know. He was very old, the Earl, wasn't he?'

Cinderella's step-mother nodded. 'But he was a good man.'

'A randy old bugger from what I hear.' The king patted her hand. 'You were too young. Your actions are forgiven.'

Esme smiled and so did Cinderella's father, and the love between the two of them shone, infecting the old king's own smile with the warmth of the man, rather than the affection of a monarch. Cinderella looked to the prince and smiled at him hoping to see some of that same glow coming back to her, but she and the prince didn't have the years of companion ship behind them – in fact, she realised, they didn't know each other at all. Her feet felt cold in her beautiful, charmless shoes.

* * *

When dinner was finally over, the king dismissed them all back to their apartments insisting that the family must be tired after their move and that Cinderella must get her beauty sleep before the preparations for the wedding began in earnest the next day. He signalled for the prince to retire with him for a nightcap.

Cinderella did not go back to her apartments. She lingered behind her family, who were intent on saying farewells to Ivy and then, as they followed her step-sister down to the courtyard where their carriage waited, Cinderella loitered in the corridor for a few minutes, then took her shoes off and crept barefoot and silent back to the drawing room. The door was open a tiny crack and she pressed her face against it. A huge fire, built with as much coal as they would be able to afford in a month, blazed in a vast grate. She heard the tinkle of liquid being poured into a glass and the heavy creak of leather as the king sat down. She could see neither her beau nor his father, but their voices drifted to her as they spoke.

'I had hoped that your recent adventures would make you grow up.' It was the king. 'But apparently not. What on earth possessed you to make a grand gesture like that? A few dances and your cock is so hard you want to marry the girl?'

'If it offends you so much father, we can call the wedding off.' The prince's voice was cold and Cinderella's heart dropped to her stomach. Surely he would fight for her? He loved her, didn't he? Surely he hadn't gone through all this searching to send her packing now? She'd be humiliated. Tears stung her eyes and she swallowed hard and willed them to pass.

'After this nonsense with that shoe, have the whole kingdom think you're a fool who can't keep his word?' The king snorted. 'No. We'll play this farce out. She's a pretty enough little thing and she'll give you heirs. I'm sure of it.' He sighed again. 'But the other one would have been a much better choice. At least she's noble. And she has a brain. She reminds me of your mother.'

'Cinderella is prettier,' the prince said. It sounded weak. From her place at the door Cinderella couldn't decide if he was defending her or himself with the statement.

'Listening at doors so early in your relationship? Where's the trust?'

A hand suddenly reached in front of her and closed the door and Cinderella jumped backwards, her heart racing. The driver, the fairy godmother's servant, leaned against the wall. He smiled but she was sure he was laughing at her. 'I didn't take you for the sort.'

'I just wanted to... I just...' She couldn't finish the sentence. 'It's none of your business anyway. And how did you get in the castle?'

'You wouldn't believe me if I told you.' Even in the gloomy corridor she could see his eyes twinkling. He folded his arms across his chest. 'So how's true love working out?'

She turned her back on him and started to walk away. She didn't have time for him now. What did he know about anything anyway? She thought he'd stayed by the door until she rounded the corner and then glanced back. She jumped again to find him right behind her.

'You're not the only one who can move silently, you know.'

Close up she could see the roughness of his tanned skin, and was struck once again by how different it was from the prince's smooth pale face. Even though she was sure he wasn't very much older than her, creases had formed on his cheeks and she wondered if they'd been made where he smiled. His dark hair flopped slightly over one eye, and she knew that, unlike his skin, it would be silky soft to the touch. He was standing so close to her she could smell him; warm and almost musky. He reminded her of the forest and all the wild things that lived there.

'What do you want?' Her voice was cold and she stood tall. He was not going to intimidate her. The king's words still rang in her head. *She's a pretty little thing.* They stung her and she wasn't entirely sure why.

'Just reminding you of your promise. To search the castle.'

'I hadn't forgotten.' Cinderella lifted her chin. He irritated her. It was the way he spoke. The way he was so confident. He irritated her *a lot.* 'I don't need a lackey to remind me.'

'Good.' This time he was the one to turn and walk away.

'I'll meet you at the back kitchen door tomorrow night at three. Don't be late.' He didn't even look back.

Cinderella crept to her room, crawled into her bed and stared at the ceiling. It was a warmer and more comfortable bed than she'd slept in for years, but she couldn't sleep. When she finally did her dreams were plagued with nightmares of running endlessly through the castle trying to find a way out.

7

'He was so very beautiful...'

O ver the next few days things seemed to get better. The prince began to court her properly and amidst the dress fittings and wedding preparations he lunched with her and walked her through the frozen maze gardens that were so beautiful, even in the grip of winter, that they almost took her breath away. They became more familiar with each other and while she told him stories of her childhood, the prince regaled her with tales of his adventures abroad. She would watch him and some times have to pinch herself that her arm was linked with his and that they were going to be married.

He kissed her often and his lips were soft on hers, but she ached to feel the passion they'd shared on the night of the Bride Ball. Much of her time though was spent learning everything that was expected from a royal bride – how to walk, how to sit, how to speak to dignitaries, how to treat servants and how to dance – while all the time having her lack of noble grace bemoaned. Oftentimes, she just wanted to cry from the effort of it, and then Rose would find her and help her and that would make her feel worse as she remembered her own selfish actions from what seemed like a lifetime ago. Her father was busy setting up the new national newspaper and her step-mother was helping him and when the two young women did see them they were full of such excited happy talk that it made the small empty space inside Cinderella grow.

She was also tired from her nightly explorations. The castle might not have been as large in reality as it always had been in her imagination but she'd begun to realise it would take her several weeks to search every room. Often she couldn't escape from dinner until after eleven, and then had to go through the pretence of going to bed before sneaking out again. She was also surprised at how many people seemed to live here. Although she was light on her feet she often had to duck behind curtains or hide beneath tables as servants or soldiers toured the building checking it was safe. What surprised her more, however, was the discovery that she found her secret task quite exciting – far more than her new life as a princess – especially when she came close to getting caught. On those nights she would arrive at the kitchen door with her face flushed and so high on the thrill that the huntsman would laugh out loud; a rough, earthy sound, and she would laugh with him even though she had nothing to report.

One night her search brought her to the prince's apartments. That afternoon they had played chess together and she had won and he'd looked at her in such surprise, as if seeing beyond the *pretty little thing* she was to the woman beneath. The woman she was growing into. Her heart had surged with the possibility that he might love her after all.

As she stood outside his bedroom, the floor cold beneath her bare feet, she couldn't help but push the door open a little to look inside. She didn't want to wake him, just to see him sleeping and imagine herself next to him, their naked bodies entwined in life as they often were in her fantasies.

The bedroom was empty and the covers still perfectly made. She stared for a long moment, the cold from the floor suddenly nothing next to the chill in her heart. Where was he? It was nearly three in the morning and he'd said at dinner that he was tired. Slowly, she closed the door. She tried to turn her mind from the only logical reason for his absence but she couldn't quite manage it. He was somewhere in the castle with another woman. She felt sick. Suddenly, she wanted her old bedroom with his picture on her wall where she could look at him and imagine him perfect. She'd been stupid. A stupid little girl. She turned and ran, her heart a little more broken.

* * *

'I still haven't found anything,' she snapped at the fairy godmother's man, waiting as he was for her by the kitchen door. 'But it would help if I knew what I was looking for.'

'Trust me,' he said. 'You'll know when you find it.'

'Trust you? I don't even know you.' She knew the words were harsh but she couldn't help it. She felt sick. Her prince was in another woman's bed. He hadn't even tried to get into hers – even after every thing at the Bride Ball. She thought of the fairy godmother. What had she said? She'd make sure Cinderella got her prince, but she couldn't guarantee true love? How arrogant she'd been to think that love wouldn't be a problem. She thought of the third dark nut tucked into the folds of her dress. What would happen if she cracked it? Would life go back to as it was before? Her stomach tightened. Even if she really wanted to – and she wasn't sure she was ready yet – she couldn't escape before fulfilling the fairy godmother's commands. She'd made a promise to search the castle. She had to see that through.

'You know me well enough. As I know you.'

'That's not true. I don't know anything about you.'

'I'm a huntsman,' he said. 'One who is very tired of royal games. Will that do?' She felt his dark eyes studying her. 'Why did you fall in love with the prince?' he asked eventually.

The question came so far out of the blue and cut through

the pain in her heart so suddenly that she found herself answering without any thought. 'He was so very beautiful.' She didn't think about the past tense. She didn't think about what that meant.

'I suppose he is, if you like that kind of thing,' the huntsman said. 'But tell me,' he leaned against the wall in his easy fashion, 'didn't you wonder for a moment how foolish and self-absorbed a man must be to only recognise the woman he claims to love from her foot fitting a shoe?'

'No,' she said, her face burning. 'No I didn't, be cause I'm a stupid, stupid girl. Is that what you want to hear?' She spat her anger at him with tears stinging her eyes, and she turned and ran back inside. She wouldn't cry in front of him. She wouldn't cry in front of anyone.

'Cinderella,' he called softly after her. She turned. He was merely a shadow in the night.

'I would have recognised you. I'd recognise you always.' The shadow moved and then he was gone, leaving Cinderella staring after him wondering what exactly he meant.

She was tucked up in her bed, her heart still heavy, when the interconnecting door opened and Rose came in, leaning on her stick.

'Where have you been?' she whispered. There was no accusation in the question, only curiosity. She walked towards the bed, and Cinderella noticed how elegantly she moved, even with her limp.

'I couldn't sleep.'

'Were you with the prince?'

The tears came then, she couldn't help it. She cried for all of them, but mainly for her and Rose and all the trouble her childish dreams had caused. 'He wasn't there,' she whispered.

She leaned against Rose who wrapped her arms around her and rocked her gently back and forth, just like she had done when they were both little girls and Cinderella couldn't sleep.

'You put too much importance on love, little sister.' Rose said. 'He is a prince and he will be a king and they always do as they please, even if they love their wives as he must love you. There are things you must learn to ignore. You will be the queen and that's what matters. You'll be the mother of his children. The rest, well, the rest of it won't really matter.' As Cinderella listened, she felt the walls of the castle close in around her. Rose made it sound so easy, this royal life. But how could you live without love? Without passion? She'd rather be dead.

'I don't know that I can,' she whispered.

'Of course you can. I'll help you.' Rose stroked Cinderella's hair as she talked, her hand running gently over the thick red curls. 'But it might do you well to love him just a little less. Life will be easier that way. You know, if you play it cleverly, you could do some good for the kingdom. Make life better for people.'

'I don't want to play anything,' Cinderella sobbed. 'I just wanted to fall in love and live in the castle.'

'Well, one out of two isn't that bad,' Rose said. 'Life isn't a fairy tale, Cinderella. I wish it was, but it isn't. And perhaps he will love you as you love him. Who can tell?"

Rose stayed in her room until she eventually fell asleep, Cinderella relishing the contact and affection. She'd been so lonely. Rose must have been too.

'I love you, Rose,' she whispered, as the knot in her stomach finally unfurled and sleep claimed her.

'I love you too, Cinderella,' her sister said.

The prince continued to be attentive to her but she found it hard to maintain her facade of joy when he was clearly keeping a lover secret from her. She checked his room twice more in the following nights and neither time was he there. She'd asked him how he slept and whether his apartments were comfortable. He always replied yes, and she kept the smile on her face even though she wanted to shout at him and call him a liar. By the third day, she took refuge in her room claiming fatigue at all the wedding preparations and ordered the maids to fill her a hot bath.

It was only when they'd left did she notice the little brown mouse that had followed them in. A scar ran along its back and she was surprised at the sudden surge of affection she felt at the sight of the little familiar creature.

'How did you get in here?' she asked. She crouched and held her hand out to it and laughed delightedly as it ran onto her palm, its tiny feet tickling against her skin. 'You're quite the little adventurer, aren't you, Mr Mouse?' She placed him carefully on a cushion on her bed. 'Maybe you should be Mrs Mouse, actually,' she said, undoing the laces of her dress. 'Women are more reliable.'

Her dress slid away to the ground and as she peeled off her undergarments it was good to feel the air on her skin. Even though it was warm, she shivered slightly with the pleasant sensation. The mouse stood up on its hind legs, its dark eyes studying her. It was a strange little thing, but she was glad of its company.

'Where do you think he goes every night?' she said, softly, lowering her naked body into the hot bath, and closing her eyes. 'Am I so terribly unlovable?' She sighed and then opened her eyes to pick up the sponge and soap. The little mouse was sitting on the edge at the other end of the large tub. It really was a remarkable little thing. She soaped the sponge and ran it over her small firm breasts and flat stomach. Her skin tingled. The prince had awoken something in her at the ball and although she was realising that love was elusive, that fire of lust still burned. 'Was it all just the shoes? Really? Why would she do that to me?' Her voice grew softer as her body responded to her own touch.

'Some fairy godmother,' she murmured as she grew lost in her fantasy.

She closed her eyes and shut out the little mouse and the castle around her and she was back on the balcony at the Bride Ball and the prince's hands were exploring her. Her hands moved across her body. In her mind, his hands were tanned this time, however, and rougher, and when he kissed her she could feel rough stubble rubbing her cheeks. She gasped as her fingers worked, imagining his mouth down between her legs, and then him moving up and inside her, and as she moved towards a climax she was surrounded by the scents of the forest.

The shouts of 'Thief! Thief! The thief has been caught!' woke her suddenly from her fantasy and, barely noticing the mouse scurrying away, she got out of the bath and wrapped a robe around her wet body before padding to the window, pulling back the thick rich curtain and looking down on the court yard below. Castle life was kept relatively quiet at the request of the queen who was always suffering from some headache or ailment or another. But this morning there was a huge amount of fuss outside as an Earl's carriage, identifiable by the blue flag hanging from the front, drew up and a fat man with impossibly thin stockinged legs climbed down awkwardly. Behind the carriage was a cart carrying what looked like a wooden cage. Cinderella frowned. Was that the prisoner? She was sure there was someone inside it.

As the Earl was escorted inside, four footmen ran down the stairs and lifted the cage down. Several of the ordinary servants and merchants who had loitered nearby rushed forward as soon as the Earl had disappeared inside. 'Thief!' one shouted at whoever was locked in the box, jabbing a stick in between the bars. 'They'll send you to the Troll Road!' The footmen shooed them back, but still the jeers and catcalls continued.

Cold flooded Cinderella's stomach. A thief. Her nerves jangled. It couldn't be, could it? There must be hundreds of thieves in the city? She pushed the window open and leaned out into the cold morning air.

'Buttons?' she called down, not caring about the heads that all tilted upwards, staring at her in her clingy robe. 'Buttons? Is that you?'

From between two bars, a pale hand appeared and waved weakly.

'Oh no,' Cinderella muttered, stumbling back wards into her room. 'Oh, no.' She grabbed at her clothes. 'Rose!' she shouted. 'Rose! Something terrible's happened!'

8

'Take the Troll Road...'

The evidence against Buttons, or Robin as it turned out was his real name, was overwhelming. Caught red-handed stealing two of the earl's silver spoons – from a collection of one hundred and twenty-three which should have been a collection of one hundred and thirty – it did not take long for the masters of various households to marry up visits from the castle boy with small items going missing. It was true in the castle itself, too, where the kitchen staff confirmed that there had been many instances of fresh loaves and cheeses vanishing along with occasional bottles of wine from the cellar. Even those items that had simply been mislaid were being added to the list of Buttons' crimes.

There was no trial to speak of. He was, after all, accused of crimes against the king. Although judges did exist for the common people – albeit the trials were always a speedy and rather haphazard affair – in this instance Buttons was dealt with behind closed doors in the presence of the king, the prince and the council of nobles. It was no surprise when he was declared guilty and sentenced to take the Troll Road.

Cinderella and Rose had waited in the corridor outside, clasping each other's hands, until the nobles in all their fur-trimmed finery filed out, already discussing the fine lunch that awaited them and Buttons' fate forgotten. The two girls looked at each other and knew what had to be done. Rose would try and talk to the king; Cinderella would tackle the prince.

Cinderella's heart was beating fast when she knocked on the apartment door and stepped inside. She was used to seeing the main bedroom at night and in the dark, merely shapes in the gloom, but the vast space was beautifully decorated in creams and whites with trim in blues and purples. She noticed her diamond shoe had been tossed carelessly on top of a wardrobe so high that it could barely be seen. She wondered when it had no longer merited the velvet cushion.

'What are you doing here?' The prince asked, surprised to see her. He was changing out of his formal clothes, and was stripped to his waist. 'Excited about the Troll Road?' He clearly was, his eyes bright and face flushed. 'Have you ever been?'

Cinderella shook her head and stared at his chest; broad and smooth and exactly how she'd imagined it in her fantasies. A silver chain glinted against his skin. She swallowed and tried to focus her thoughts. 'No, I'm not excited. I'm here to plead for mercy for the servant boy.'

'What?' he frowned. 'You are joking, aren't you? He's a thief. What does he matter to you?

'He's just a boy,' she said. 'And he didn't steal any thing too terrible.'

'How would you know?'

'I... well, I knew him. Sort of.' A flush crept up her face. 'He sometimes brought me things. Coal when it was cold. He gave other people things too.'

'I didn't realise your mother's marriage had taken her so low that you were relying on gifts from dishonest servants.'

'I don't think he thought he was doing any harm. He's a good...'

'Shut up.' The prince's face hardened as he cut her off, his mouth tightening into a thin line. He didn't look so handsome anymore. 'He stole from *us*. He will go to the Troll Road and you will sit beside me as he drops. And you will never say another word about him to me. Do you understand?'

'But—'

'You need to stop behaving like a commoner,' he muttered, pulling a fresh shirt over his head. 'And talking like one. Your voice – it's very coarse. Concentrate on the elocution lessons and leave matters of royal justice to my father and I.'

His words stung. She hadn't thought he could hurt her any more than his cooling affections had done, but seeing his avoidance of her writ large on his face and hearing his words made her want to weep all over again.

'Why are you marrying me?' she asked, quietly. 'You don't love me.'

'I have to.' He looked at her and she saw sadness in his eyes, and she wondered who exactly it was for. 'The whole kingdom is expecting it. If I put you aside now I will look heartless and fickle.'

'Maybe I should leave,' Cinderella said. She found that, after all her childish dreams of living in the castle, the idea of returning to her old home wasn't so terrible after all. Even with the cold and the meagre amounts of food.

'You can't. I'm the prince and you're a commoner. How much more foolish would I look if you were to go?'

'I thought you wanted me,' she said, and a tear slipped down her cheek. She didn't know what to do. How was this going to be any kind of life?

'I don't know what happened on those nights of the Bride Ball.' The prince slumped into a chair as Cinderella sat on the edge of the bed and they looked at each other, this time as honest strangers rather than supposed lovebirds. 'I wasn't looking for love. I was done with beauty. I wanted to find a practical wife; someone my father would approve of.

Someone who understood what being a queen would entail.' He looked over at Cinderella. 'My mother was a noble and she still finds it difficult.'

Cinderella thought once again of Rose, her cool head and warm heart and sense of distance from the world. Rose had never talked of boys or crushes or hung the prince's picture on the wall.

'And then there you were,' he said, and shrugged. 'And from the moment I saw you until the moment they found you, I was driven with a desire I've never known. I thought I loved you. I would have died for you. But then when you arrived here, it was all different.'

'That...' Cinderella struggled to find the right word, '...that passion we felt on the balcony, though, surely that's still there?'

'You're like a perfect copy of that girl. I *should* want you. You're beautiful. When I look at you I'm reminded of how I felt that night and yet none of it is there. I can't make myself want you.'

Cinderella stared down at her shoes; blue satin to match her dress, but no magic in them to light a fire in this man she'd been so convinced was her destiny.

'What will we do?' she asked.

'It will get better.' He leaned forward and squeezed her hand. 'You will want for nothing. You will have a good life.' With each sentence Cinderella could feel the walls of the castle tightening around her. His voice hardened and he straightened up, as if only by touching her, he'd felt repulsed. 'But you will behave like a queen and you will come to the Troll Road with me at dusk tomorrow.' Cinderella felt her in sides crumble. She couldn't help Buttons. She had no power to.

Rose had no better luck with the king who wasn't even interested in Rose's point that perhaps he had been doing some good with the things he'd taken. A thief was a thief, and the earl was angry. The king would not take the side of a serving boy over a man he relied on for funds and bodies in times of battle. Buttons was going to the Troll Road and there would be a royal procession there to remind the people that although he was a generous king, his justice was also to be feared.

That night, Cinderella's search was half-hearted. She looked through libraries and studies, filled with books on law and science, where the kings' secretaries drafted new laws and old. She went down to the kitchens and wine cellars but people were still working there, the heart of the castle never really slept, but while she looked she figured that if there were something strange hidden here that her wicked fairy godmother – as she'd come to think of her – was so keen on having, it wouldn't be kept in a place where all and sundry passed by. Her head and heart were filled with thoughts of poor Buttons, locked up in the dungeons with no chance of mercy. He had been so kind to her and others and yet none would step forward to save him. How could they if even Cinderella and Rose couldn't get the king or the prince to intervene. The castle sank into slumber as three o'clock rolled around again and she crept through the narrow corridors at the back of the kitchens until she reached the small back door.

The huntsman was waiting, as he always was. Cinderella was surprised at how relieved she was to see him, and he listened as she blurted out Buttons' fate. He didn't speak until she was finished and then stared into the night, where somewhere an owl hooted.

'The Troll Road,' he said, thoughtfully.

'He'll never survive. No one ever does.' Cinderella thought of all the gifts Buttons had brought. Gifts she'd taken so lightly, without seeing this eventual consequence in the cheeky young man's future. She'd wanted his stories and the game he played for her and hadn't paid attention to the risks he'd been taking. How stupid had she been? Her old life was only a few weeks gone at most, but it felt like a lifetime ago. 'We need to help him.' She looked at the strange man who'd become her nightly companion. 'Surely you can help him? Could we break him out of the dungeons? Give him some money and food and send him to the forest? We'd need a distraction, of course, and maybe some more people to help, but if you have friends...'

'The mouse,' he said, cutting her off. His voice was low

and his eyes thoughtful as the winter wind lifted his dark hair. 'Get the mouse to him and tell him to keep it in his pocket until they drop him from the bridge.'

'What mouse?' Cinderella frowned. What was he talking about? 'Can't *you* do something?'

'The mouse that's been following you around. *That* mouse. And I am doing something.' He leaned into the doorway, standing close to her. 'You just have to trust me.'

And she found, much as it irked her, that she did.

Dusk was falling as Cinderella picked up the little mouse and tucked him into the bodice of her dress along with a purple silk handkerchief as Rose looked on horrified, leaning on her walking stick. 'What on earth are you doing?'

'I'm not entirely sure.' The mouse wriggled against her breast and Cinderella loosened the ribbons at the front of her dress just in case he was suffocating. He was tickling, that was for sure. 'I'm going to give it to Buttons. Apparently it might help him.'

Rose picked up her heavy fur coat and slid her arms inside. 'You do know what a troll is, don't you? I don't think it's going to be scared of a mouse. Who told you that anyway?'

'A friend.' She tried to be nonchalant but it didn't work. Rose paused and then picked up Cinderella's own pale fur and wrapped it around her shoulders.

'Darling Cinderella, we don't have any friends.' She smiled. 'But I hope whoever this person is, they know something we don't.'

'Me too.' She looked out of the window to the procession gathering below. It was going to be a fine affair, she thought. If only the purpose wasn't so deadly. Beyond the castle walls she could see the route to the bridge lit up by great torches which sank the rest of the city into shade. The route would be lined by smiling people too, caught up in the excitement of seeing royalty and feeding the frenzy. Beautiful and terrifying, that's how the lights looked to her. She wondered how poor Buttons was coping.

'We need to go,' Rose said, pulling open the bedroom door. 'They'll be waiting for you.'

Out in the courtyard Rose found their parents alongside Ivy and the Viscount in the throng and stood with them, and Cinderella was pleased to see that they looked sombre and clearly were not caught up in the excitement of it as so many others were. Side by side, her step-mother and Rose looked elegantly aloof, as she imagined all noble women should, and even her father had taken on an air of sophistication. His back was straighter too, now he had a newspaper to run again. She wondered how he'd report this?

She nodded and gave them a small smile and they smiled back and for the thousandth time she wished she'd realised how lucky she was to have her family at all instead of living in her fantasies about a dead mother and having a royal lover.

A hush fell across the gathering as chains creaked and cogs ground against each and as the prisoner was brought up in the lift from the dungeons so far below. Cinderella didn't know if it was her imagination but the night seemed to fill with a stench of rot and damp as if the air coming up with the cage hadn't been fresh in a long, long time. Ahead she could see her grey pony, a gift from her fiancé, waiting to be mounted, and as the torch-bearers and servants pulled back, she found she was almost alone when the gate opened. Buttons stood there, squinting even though it was nearly dark, with a fearsome, chainmailed guard on either side of him. They pushed him forward. His hands were tied in front of him and he stumbled but didn't fall. The crowd jeered slightly.

'Wait!' Cinderella called, as they were about to haul him onto the back of a cart for the cold journey to his fate. All eyes turned to her. The prince, already on horseback, started to call something out to her, but the king grabbed his arm. To reprimand his bride to be in public would not be chivalrous.

She drew herself up tall and walked towards Buttons. As she reached him, she pulled the mouse and silk handkerchief from their spot, nestled against her thumping heart.

'A king must be just, and justice must be served,' she said, her voice ringing loud and clear across the impatient crowd in the courtyard, whinnying horses and stamping boots. 'But a princess must be gentle and kind. And so, to honour my husband to be and his majesty the king, I offer this traitor a good luck token' – she held her hand up for a moment and then thrust the contents into Buttons' pocket – 'and wish him a swift and painless end.' She held Buttons' gaze for a moment before whispering in a rush, 'Keep it with you.' He gave her the tiniest nod in reply.

The mouse delivered, Cinderella turned back to face the king and fell into a low curtsey, before walking towards her waiting pony.

'Your gesture is most becoming of a royal princess,' the king nodded at her. Even the prince gave her a half smile. She reserved her own for a glance at Rose, standing at the castle wall to see the procession off, who beamed approvingly back. Cinderella was definitely getting better at the game.

She didn't look at Buttons once during the procession through the streets, and pulled her fur-lined hood over her head so no one could see she didn't share the excitement of the rest of the parade. People jeered as the cart went by and every now and then something rotten was thrown his way, hitting the poor, cold boy. Even though he was on his way to his death they seemed to want to punish him more. She scanned the crowds, lit up as they were by the high burning torches on the path, and wondered how many of them Buttons had helped with gifts of food or money when times were desperate. Perhaps they were the most aggressive in their shouting for fear that he might give up their names as the bridge grew closer.

Finally they reached the edge of the city and the bridge loomed ahead of them, the forest dark on the other side. Cinderella's stomach twisted as she saw the thick stone rising up from the overgrown banks of the dead river below. Her father and step-mother had never brought them here as children and neither had she been one of those who'd come to play at being prisoners and trolls near its edge before get ting shooed away by the soldiers who guarded it. The bridge was wider than she'd expected, maybe twenty feet across, and as soon as the heavily armoured bridge keeper leaned over the side and lit the torches that hung there, a fearsome growling rumbled from underneath, so deep and angry she was sure the ground beneath her horse's feet trembled with it.

They took Buttons down from the cart, and the royal procession watched in silence as he was delivered into the Bridge Guard's hands. He looked tiny between them. The Bridge Guard were known for their size and fearsome, silent natures, and all that could be seen below their helmets were their beards. Cinderella thought they looked like armoured bears, and she shivered seeing her friend between them. Buttons did not look her way, but she was proud to see that he wasn't crying nor begging for mercy. His eyes were defiant.

The troll roared again, knowing fresh meat was coming

its way, and Cinderella flinched. What had the huntsman been thinking? How could a mouse be any use against such a creature?

The night was dark around them, dusk having been eaten up in the hour's walk to the bridge, and as Buttons, his hands untied, walked into the middle of the bridge, Cinderella wished all the torches would fail so she wouldn't have to watch.

'You have been found guilty of theft and treason,' the crier called out to him. 'Do you have anything to say before the sentence is carried out?'

In the flickering light, Buttons simply smiled. It was his cheeky grin, the one she'd taken so much for granted in their friendship. A brave smile. He'd known what risks he was taking all along and it hadn't stopped him. She hadn't paid attention to his words of warning about castle life but now she understood. She'd only seen him as a boy, but he'd been far more grown up than she was.

'I'll be back for more silver,' Buttons said. 'There's plenty to go round and people are hungry.' He looked down at his feet. 'Not as hungry as the troll sounds, mind you, but maybe I won't be to his taste.'

'Do it,' the king growled, unimpressed by this lack of repentance from his subject.

Buttons pulled the handkerchief and the mouse out of his pocket and his smile fell as he looked down confused.

Cinderella strained to see. Something was happening there – something was changing.

The largest of the Bridge Guard tugged at a heavy wooden lever at the edge of the bank, and it squealed at being forced out of winter's grip and into use. The trapdoor opened and Buttons fell, vanishing from sight to the dead riverbed below. The troll roared. And then roared some more.

'Please,' Cinderella rested her hand on the prince's arm. 'Can we leave now?' If she was forced to hear poor Buttons screaming then it would tear her heart apart.

'Of course we're leaving,' the prince said, already turning his horse around. 'We're not barbaric.' Cinderella looked into his perfectly beautiful face and wondered if he had any idea how ridiculous that sounded after what they'd just done.

9

'A secret'

Dinner was waiting for them at the castle, but Cinderella couldn't eat. Instead she pushed her food around her plate until it made a heap at one side that wasn't fooling anyone, but unlike when she was a child and food was scarce, no one told her off or forced her to eat it. She wondered perhaps if it was simply that no one noticed. The prince and the king were talking and laughing and the queen just smiled occasionally and commented on the fine quality of the venison and how she hoped the weather would break soon and they could all get back to the hunt.

Cinderella's insides churned as a servant took her plate away. She itched to see the huntsman and hear about his plan to save Buttons. Had it even been possible? There were always rumours of people surviving taking the Troll Road and escaping to the forest, but as far as she knew none of them had ever returned to the city, so it was all just myth and legend. The huntsman wouldn't come until three and that was four long hours away. Time that she should spend searching the castle for whatever it was the fairy godmother was so keen for her to find. She'd been through so many of the rooms she was sure she'd never find whatever it was, and what then? Would the fairy godmother transport *her* to the Troll Road for her uselessness? The way their bargain had turned out she wouldn't be surprised. She looked across the mahogany table to the prince whose face was ever more handsome in the candlelight.

She also wanted to know where he disappeared to every night. Was it something as simple as a serving girl? Or one of the other ladies of the court? She wondered why she cared – for all her worry about his feelings towards her, she hadn't really taken much time to think about how her feelings for him had changed. Had it ever been more than a childish crush? She'd fallen in love with a picture and a dream. The reality was different. Still, the image of his empty bedroom stuck in her mind and her curiosity was beginning to overwhelm her.

She'd follow him, she decided, as the apple pie arrived laced with Chantilly cream. The scent of sweet apples was like perfume in the air and her mouth suddenly watered. Following the prince and searching the castle weren't necessarily different things – especially if he was going somewhere she hadn't yet explored. She bit into the pie and the pastry melted on her tongue and cinnamon apple exploded sharply on her tongue. That's what she'd do. She'd follow him.

After dinner, while the king and the prince drank brandy and discussed whatever it was men talked about when women weren't present, Cinderella ran back to her room and breathlessly changed out of her stiff formal dress into a looser, lighter one that she could move quickly and quietly in. Barefoot, she made her way back to the drawing room and hid behind a thick curtain, peering through the gap at the double doors. She didn't have to wait long before the prince came out, nodding a polite goodnight to his father and leaving the king to the fire and the quiet and his thoughts.

Cinderella saw his shoulders slump as soon as the door closed and he paused for a moment before walking away. She gave him a head start and then crept out from between the curtains and followed, staying close to the walls. It was late and most of the castle was sleeping or in their rooms; the only sound was the click of his heels on marble echoing as she snuck along behind him.

Her heart sank as they reached his apartments, Cinderella still on the stairs, peering with one eye round the wall to watch him. He'd stopped outside his door. Was this going to be the first night he actually went to bed? Surely it couldn't be? Surely—

The prince leaned his forehead against the closed door and took a deep breath as if battling some in ternal dilemma. Cinderella's heart raced as his jaw clenched and he stood up tall. What was plaguing him? Surely if he was just sleeping with a serving girl that wouldn't cause any inner crisis. Unless he was beginning to fall in love with Cinderella, of course. Her heart leapt slightly at that. Even if she wasn't sure that she loved him, she wanted him to love her. He sighed again, tapped his head gently against the wood two times and then turned away. Cinderella crept after him.

The servants' quarters – with the exception of the king and queen's personal maids and footmen – were mainly located in the lower levels of the castle, and that was where Cinderella had expected them to head. The prince, however, didn't lead her down into that hubbub of warmth and life. Instead, he walked steadily, with a sense of purpose rather than urgency, along several corridors that twisted and turned and then led into the heart of the building. It seemed far from the places that Cinderella knew, where windows let in so much light. This part of the castle she'd never seen before. She wondered how many months she'd have taken to find it herself.

The corridors were darker, only occasional lamps lit on the walls, and here and there statues and pictures had been covered to protect them from dust. The air was cold and smelt slightly of damp as if no fires had been lit in the surrounding rooms for years. The prince's shadow stretched long behind him and Cinderella let it guide her in his wake. She wondered for a moment what would happen if she lost him? Would she ever find her way back to the castle that she knew? Or would she wander these rooms screaming until she died? She wished she'd taken a hunk of bread from dinner and left a trail of bread-crumbs to follow should she need to. She shivered and crept closer. She wouldn't lose him. She didn't have a choice.

Finally they came to a spiral stone stairwell and the prince began to climb it, Cinderella behind him. They climbed for several minutes and Cinderella hoped the prince wouldn't hear her breathing as it became more laboured. There were no lights here, but a cold breeze zigzagged in the small space, and here and there tiny holes had been cut into the thick stone, perhaps for bowmen to shoot through a long time ago when the kingdoms were still to learn to keep their battles away from their capitals. Through them, shards of moonlight landed on patches of stone and Cinderella caught glimpses of abstract parts of the prince's body; a leg, a shoe, a slice of torso, as the air grew colder and the stairs turned into a level floor.

She'd thought they must be in one of the turrets, but instead it was another corridor. There was no pretence at decoration here, however, the walls only hung with cobwebs that extended from their corners, covered in dust. Grit dug into her bare feet as she hid in the shadows and watched the prince as he finally came to a halt outside a door. Unlike the others they'd passed this one had been polished recently, the dark wood shining and the iron that studded it black and gleaming. The prince reached around his neck and undid a chain. A gold key glinted in the gloom and Cinderella pressed herself against the wall as he glanced around before sliding it into the lock.

The door swung open and then he was gone. Cinderella scurried forward in time to hear the grating of metal on metal as he locked the room once again from the inside. Her heart thumped and she pressed her eye to the tiny gaps where the hinges sat. What was he doing in there? What did he have in there that was so precious he'd locked it up so far from the central hub of the castle? He was the prince – surely he didn't have to worry about anything being stolen? Why hide whatever it was? And why only visit in the middle of the night when everyone was asleep? She could see nothing through the tiny gap and pressed her ear against it instead. She could hear something; the scrape of a chair, and then his voice. He was talking, but she couldn't make out his words. She frowned and listened harder, holding her breath. There was only one voice: his. Who or what was he talking to?

She stared at the door wishing she could see through the wood. What was in there that was making him so secretive?

A secret.

That's why he kept the key around his neck. That's why he only came in the middle of the night. And that was why he kept whatever it was in this forgotten part of the castle. The king didn't know about it. No one did. Her face flushed with excitement. Could this be what the fairy godmother had wanted her to find?

She shivered in the quiet and the cold for an hour, listening to his voice burbling through the wood and then, when the key turned in the lock again, she darted back to the shadows, this time on the far side. Her hiding place didn't matter. He was lost in his own thoughts when he emerged, and as soon as he'd secured the room he placed the key on its chain back round his neck and tucked it under his shirt before heading back towards the stairs, oblivious of Cinderella behind him.

This time she paid attention to the journey. Her searching of the castle had honed her directional skills and at every turning they made she logged some small landmark, whether it be a covered picture or a crack in the paintwork on the walls. Finally, the lights grew brighter and she recognised her surroundings.

She stopped and allowed the prince to slip away from her, knowing that he would be going back to his bedroom. Whatever need had driven him was sated by the secret contents of that locked room.

Somewhere a clock chimed as if to welcome her back to the world of warmth and light and beauty. It struck three times. The huntsman would be waiting. Her heart leapt and she raced down the stairs, red hair flying out behind her, flames against the wall. Perhaps he'd have good news of Buttons. And she had news of her own.

She arrived at the back door breathless and yanked it open. He was leaning against the wall, just as he always was.

'I think I've found something! There's a room! Somewhere forgotten! And he keeps the key around his neck. The prince! It's where he goes at night. Do you think that's what she wants?'

She was dancing from foot to foot with excitement and it took a moment for her to realise something was wrong. The huntsman was leaning against the wall, that was true, but not with his normal laconic elegance. His head was down and one arm clutched against his side where a dark stain was spreading through his clothes. Her stomach shrank into the pit of her belly.

'What happened?' She stepped outside, not caring about the icy cold that stung her bare feet. 'You're hurt.' Finally, he looked up.

'I'll be okay.'

His eyes were black with pain and his mouth pressed tight. Blood stained the side of his face.

'No, you won't.' Without thinking she pulled one of his

arms around her shoulder. 'Come on.' He was heavy against her, using all his strength to stay on his feet, and she tried to murmur encouragement to him as they negotiated the route back up to her bedroom. In the light she could see that half of his tunic was sodden with blood and his tanned skin was pale. She choked back tears that suddenly sprang hot in the back of her eyes. The huntsman was always *there*. He couldn't die. He just couldn't.

Thankful it was the dead of night, they finally made it to her apartments and once inside she locked the door behind them.

'I shouldn't be here,' he muttered.

'Shut up,' she said. 'And take your shirt off.'

He gave her a half smile and raised an eyebrow. 'You might not get my best performance but I'm willing to give it a shot.'

'Just do it.' She flashed him an angry look, but inside her heart leapt. He wasn't dying at least. Badly injured perhaps, but not dying.

She filled a pan of water from the large jug on her table and hung it over the fire to warm, before turning the lights down and creeping through the connecting door into Rose's room.

Rose rolled over and murmured, but didn't wake, and Cinderella checked her drawers as quietly as possible until she found the box of bandages and salves she knew Rose would have, exactly as she always had in their old house for every time Cinderella fell or scraped her knee or banged her head while playing. She silently thanked her step-sister and crept back to her own room, closing the door behind her.

She left the lighting soft in case it would creep under the door and wake Rose and fetched the warm water. The huntsman had peeled his filthy shirt off and she could see the gash that ran up his side, his skin pulled apart and his flesh exposed. Thankfully it didn't look too deep. She took a soft towel from the table and dipped it in the water, carefully starting to wipe the blood from his chest. His skin was tanned and the muscles in his stomach twitched as the cloth touched him. The prince's chest was pale and smooth. The huntsman's was tanned and scarred and dark hair curled across his sternum. She wondered what it would be like to run her fingers through it and feel the strong muscles underneath, and she swallowed involuntarily as a heat flooded through her body that had nothing to do with the fire. She could feel him watching her as she washed the edges of his wound, the atmosphere between them suddenly electric.

'What happened?' she asked, desperate to break it. She dipped her fingers in the pot of salve and smoothed it over the long cut. His skin was warm beneath her touch and he gasped and swore under his breath.

'Don't be a child,' she said, and smiled up at him from her place on the floor and for the first time she realised how very handsome he was. She didn't know what she felt about him, this stranger. Some times she was sure she didn't like him very much at all, and yet her heart was beating so fast she thought it would burst out of her chest. Her skin tingled with a sudden urge to feel his hands on her. 'Tell me what happened,' she said again, wiping her hands.

'It doesn't matter.' The huntsman pressed a pad against his wound and held the end of the bandage against his stomach as she passed it round his back and wound it tight against the dressed wound. 'All that matters is that your friend is safe. He's in the woods.'

'Buttons?' Cinderella looked up. 'But how...' The questioned drained away as she thought of the gash on his side. It hadn't been from a knife or a sword, it was too ragged at the edges. A claw, however...

'*You* fought the troll?' She got to her feet and stared at him as he tucked the end of the abandoned bandage away and stood up.

'Sadly I didn't kill it.'

'But I don't understand. How did you get past the guards? How did you—?'

'It doesn't matter,' he said.

He stood up, and they were so close the bodice of her dress was nearly brushing his bare skin.

'You saved him?' she said. She was breathless. She couldn't help it. She felt like she had on the balcony at the

Bride Ball but this time there were no charmed slippers to encourage the heat.

'You wanted me to.' His voice was cracked slightly and as his eyes travelled over her face she knew he felt the same passion she did. He reached for her, one hand sliding round her neck, the touch of his rough fingers sending sparks through her whole body, and he wrapped them in her hair. He spun her round so quickly she gasped. They were facing the large, ornate mirror that hung almost the length of the wall.

'I want to watch you,' he breathed into her neck. He held her tight against him and she was sure if he'd let go, her legs would give way beneath her. 'I want *you* to watch you. See the woman you are.' Their eyes locked in the mirror and he lowered his mouth, tracing his lips against her neck as one hand undid the laces at the front of her dress. She moaned and her head tilted sideways, as he breathed on her, barely touching her with his lips and tongue, as his fingers expertly sought out her nipple, teasing it, all the time his dark eyes watching her reactions from beneath the hood of his soft, dark hair. She pressed back into him feeling the hardness there and she reached a hand behind her to touch him. He grabbed her wrist firmly and stopped her, smiling at her reflection.

'Slowly, princess,' he whispered.

'I want you to kiss me,' she said, breaking his hold and twisting round to face him. Her dress was falling free, and he stared at her for a moment and then pushed her up against the mirror. Her arms slid round his waist and she ran her fingers up his naked spine. She could feel scar tissue breaking the smoothness of his skin and her stomach tingled all the more for it. This was no spoilt prince. This was a man who'd fought a monster because she asked him for help. He ran one hand up over her breast and to her neck, pinning her firmly against the glass. As their lips moved so close together she could feel the warmth of his breath and the strength of his hand and she thought she would explode. She gripped his back, the strange skin of the long scar on his back heightening her excitement and then, out of nowhere, her head was filled with the image of brown fur. A twitching nose.

Scar tissue. On his back. The troll.

Oh no. Oh no, it couldn't be. Could it?

'Wait just one minute.' Just as his lips had been about to brush hers, she pushed him away, the pressure of her hand touching his bandaged side enough to make him gasp and pull back.

'What? What's the matter?'

She stared at him as the realisation dawned on her. 'You've got a scar on your back.'

'So what?'

'Just like the mouse. The one you insisted I give Buttons.' Surely it couldn't be? But the mouse had always been so odd, following first Buttons and then her. What kind of field mouse did that? She raised one shaking finger at him. 'You're the mouse, aren't you? That's how you got to the troll.'

He stared at her and then shrugged. 'She cursed me. And then when she needed me, she half-lifted it. Man by night, mouse by day.'

'The fairy godmother?' Cinderella's eyes widened.

'If that's what you want to call her. She's a queen, and she can be a bitch.'

'But why? I mean... what did you do? And...' Her head was filled with questions which were abruptly crushed by the sudden weight of memories. 'Oh god,' she wheezed, suddenly almost unable to breathe with the horror of it. 'You've seen me naked. You watched me in the bath.' Her eyes widened. 'I put you down my top!' She stared at him. 'You bastard.'

She turned away and covered her mouth as another memory dawned. Buttons. The mouse had been there when Buttons... 'My kitchen. You *saw*... you watched...'

'What was I supposed to do?' he said, the start of a smile twinkling in his eyes.

'Close your eyes at least? Run away.'

'I'm a hot-blooded man,' he grinned, a lopsided, infuriatingly handsome expression. 'To be fair, inside your dress it was too dark to see anything. But the bath, and Buttons well, that was amazing... what could I do?'

She let out some sound halfway between a growl and a shriek and slapped him hard across the face. He was unbelievable! How could she even have thought about

144

kissing him? Had she forgotten how much he irritated her? She stormed to the door and unlocked it with shaking hands. 'Get out,' she said. 'And get me the other slipper back from that witch.'

'What do you need the slipper for?' He frowned slightly.

'Just get it. Then she can have her prize and then we can both be free of that woman's meddling.' She glowered at him. 'And of each other.'

'Fine,' he strode towards her, his jaw locked. She wasn't sure if it was in pain or anger or lust and she didn't care. He was impossible. He was uncouth. What had she been thinking? She had almost kissed him! He stopped before her, in the doorway, and her heart started racing again despite herself. 'If that's what you want,' he said. 'Next time you need someone saving from a troll do it yourself.'

She pushed him out of the door and locked it again, her breathing loud and angry, before throwing her self down on the bed like she used to as a teenager. She wanted to cry with the shame of it. How could he have just sat on the side of the bath and watched her doing *that*? He must have been laughing at her. God, she'd been so stupid. She punched the pillow and then buried her face in it. She hated him. She really, really did.

10

'She'd finish it once and for all...'

*S*he'd covered the mirrors over, for once wanting some complete quiet so she could think. There was nothing to see anyway. Black ice and slush filling the roads. The occasional tradesman heading to work early; bakers and butchers determined to catch what trade they could. She needed to lift the winter spell soon, but it came from a dark place in her soul that had a life of its own and was difficult to manage. But the people would need to eat and there was only so much ore the exhausted dwarves could mine in order to trade for grain. The kingdom – her kingdom – needed to thrive again and she had to make it happen. Yet she couldn't make the ice inside herself melt, so how was she supposed to save the land?

But maybe things would change soon. Perhaps they

already were. Outside, the sky was turning from black to blue with hints of purple as dawn bruised the horizon. For once there were no heavy clouds gathering at the start of a new day, as if the shivers of excitement she'd felt had swept them away. She drank more wine and stared out at nothing. She knew she should steel herself for disappointment but she couldn't help the warmth in the pit of her stomach. Her heart thumped hard against her ribs. It had been doing so for hours, ever since the huntsman arrived, frozen and exhausted, and asked for the slipper. He'd been wounded but wouldn't say how, and refused help from her medical men. He'd been bandaged well enough, he said. By better hands than anything she could offer. She didn't argue with him. It would take far more than a flesh wound to kill off the huntsman.

The slipper.

The girl wanted the slipper. Lilith had frozen at that and for a moment all the servants in the castle had inadvertently shivered as if someone had walked over their graves. The huntsman said Cinderella hadn't told him what her plan was, only that she'd found a secret room and the prince had the key to it. She'd smiled at that. It hadn't taken the girl too long to realise that if you're going to hunt for something hidden, you first look for some one who's hiding something. Her charming prince hadn't managed to love her for long, it seemed.

She gave the huntsman the slipper and lifted the curse

for long enough to send him back with it. He'd get twenty-four hours as a man; then he'd turn back into a mouse again forever. That, however, was his problem not hers.

The minutes were ticking by eternally slowly. She wondered how far he'd got on his journey. She wondered what would happen when he gave her the slipper and Cinderella got into the locked room. Mainly she wondered if this could really be it. The end of her long search. Restless, she got to her feet and wandered into the warmer ante-chamber where all her treasures were laid out. She hoped for the comfort they normally brought her but felt nothing. In the far corner the cabinet door creaked open.

'She truly is the most beautiful in all the land...'

She didn't bother trying to shut the thing up. It was pointless. Instead, she put down her wine glass and walked with more purpose than she had in a long time to the stairs leading down to the heart of the castle. She would wait for them at the edge of the kingdom. It would be safer that way, depending on the outcome, and it was time she got out into the world. And if the huntsman's girl really had found the prize after all this time then she'd finish it once and for all.

It was cold and crisp but, for the first time in a long time, the sun shone over the kingdom that day as the queen with no mercy rode into the forest.

11

'I can take care of myself...'

It was late afternoon and Cinderella had just finished retracing her steps of the previous night, making small marks on the walls with a piece of chalk at regular intervals just to make sure she didn't take a wrong turn later, when she bumped into Rose in the corridor at the base of the stairs.

'I've been looking for you everywhere,' Rose said, frowning. 'You missed lunch with father and mother. They're worried about you.' The wooden cane she'd been using had been replaced by a slender silver one but she was barely leaning on it at all. The king had sent for the finest shoe-makers in the land and they had worked tirelessly to make her beautiful shoes that helped her balance. It didn't stop Cinderella feeling guilty whenever she saw her. If she hadn't been so selfish and stupid then it would be Rose preparing for a royal wedding, her family would be financially secure, and she herself would be free.

'Sorry,' she said, trying to nonchalantly edge Rose away from the stairwell. 'I forgot. How are they?'

'They're fine. Surprisingly so. I think what happened with my foot... well, it sobered mother up.' She smiled. 'Don't get me wrong, she's happy to be back at court, but I think she's more excited about father setting up the newspaper again.'

Cinderella smiled absently, but her mind was already racing ahead. What time would the huntsman be back? Would he have the slipper? But more and more her thoughts were filled with wanting to know exactly what the prince kept behind that locked door. 'Oh,' she said, her voice dropping to a whisper. 'I think Buttons is safe. He's in the woods.'

'How do you know?' Rose's eyes widened. 'Are you sure?'

'Yes, my friend told me.' Some kind of friend, Cinderella thought. She could still die of shame when she thought about what she'd done so brazenly in front of him. She could only hope that mice didn't have very good eyesight. She began to walk away knowing that whatever secrets she was involved in she still had a teacher waiting for her in the music room who was determined to force a delicate melody from her fingers, which were proving remarkably defiant. After that it would be poetry recital practice. Both, she'd discovered, bored her to tears. Being a noble woman wasn't quite the life of love and laughter she'd fantasised about.

'Cinderella,' Rose called after her, and she stopped and turned.

'What?'

'What is going on? I know all this wedding planning must be overwhelming for you, but what are you hiding from me?' Rose had one hand on the hip of her plum dress. 'I went into your room to find you and there was some blood on your rug. And you've been in my medical kit.'

'Don't go in my room!' Cinderella snapped. Her skin burned. She hadn't even checked the carpets for drops of the huntsman's blood – she'd been too angry with him to think so practically. She'd need to find time to clean that up. The servants wouldn't say any thing, but it was better to be safe than sorry.

'I'm just worried,' Rose recoiled slightly. 'That's all.'

'I'm sorry,' Cinderella said. She didn't want to upset Rose. She'd done her enough harm already which she would never be able to put right. 'I didn't mean to sound so harsh. I'm fine. I really am.'

Rose said nothing but she still looked suspicious. Cinderella turned and headed fast down the corridor before any more questions came. She didn't want to lie, not if she didn't have to, but she didn't want to involve Rose either. This was her problem, she was going to deal with it by herself and she'd do what ever it took to get into that room. She was marrying the man anyway, so she would have to do

SARAH PINBOROUGH

it at some point, and it wasn't that long ago that she'd been desperate to be alone with him. Still, her stomach twisted nervously. It all sounded good in theory. But how would it go in practice? She pushed the worry out of her head. If the huntsman didn't come back with the slipper then it would all amount to nothing in the end.

He came as she was dressing for dinner. She'd styled her hair as she'd worn it for the Bride Ball, her face was powdered and painted and she was perfuming her skin when the knock on the door came. She pulled a robe on and opened it. There he was. Heat rushed to her face and her heart thumped. She lifted her chin. She had nothing to be ashamed of. He was the one who should be embarrassed.

'Where did you get that?' she asked, looking at the footman livery he was wearing.

'Don't worry, no one got hurt,' he answered, stepping inside. 'Men in taverns, however, should be more careful where they leave their uniforms when they get distracted by a warm body,'

'Have you got it?' she asked.

He held up a small brown bag and flinched slightly. His injury was clearly still causing him a lot of pain and her heart softened slightly. 'Why don't you sit down?' she nodded towards the chair. He did as he was told and she opened the bag and pulled the diamond shoe out.

'You look like you're getting ready to go into battle,' he said, his eyes studying her.

'Battle?'

'All the war paint.'

'Are you trying to insult me?' Anger flared up in her stomach again. Why did she find him so confusing? He'd risked his life to save Buttons because she'd asked him to, and yet he could be so infuriating. She always felt so uncomfortable under his gaze. Why was that?

'No, you look beautiful,' he said. 'I'm just curious about all this effort for dinner. And what you're planning to do with that slipper.'

Cinderella sat at her dressing table with her back to him. It was just easier that way.

'I know where the second slipper is,' she said, fixing a diamond necklace around her neck. 'And I need to get the key.'

'Which he keeps on a chain under his shirt,' the huntsman said dryly.

Cinderella's back stiffened slightly. 'That's right.'

There was a long pause. 'I see,' he said.

'I'll wait until he's asleep and then steal it. We can get whatever's in there and then we're done.' She skipped over the meat of her plan. Why did she suddenly feel awkward? And – if she was honest with herself – more than a little bit scared?

'You've got it all figured out then,' the huntsman said.

'Yes.' She swallowed hard. 'Anyway, you should go. I need to get dressed.'

Behind her, he pulled himself to his feet. 'Why bother?' he asked. 'Clothes don't seem to be part of your plan.'

His words stung but she didn't turn round as he limped towards the door.

'But as long as you know what you're doing,' he said. 'It's not my business.'

'I can take care of myself,' she snapped. Tears sprung to the back of her eyes suddenly and out of nowhere. How else did he expect her to get the key from the prince and then return it without it being noticed? And he was her husband to be. It was hardly... well, hardly like the things the girls in the taverns – girls the huntsman no doubt spent all his time with – did.

'I'll take your word for it,' he said, and then the door closed behind him and he was gone. Cinderella stared at her reflection and her whole body trembled for several minutes; anger, unhappiness and something else she couldn't quite figure out all roiling into a storm of emotion inside her.

War paint. Maybe it was. She certainly didn't recognise the woman staring back at her from the mirror. A lady of the court with tamed and lacquered hair and painted features. Still, she thought. Perhaps it was best to think of herself as someone else for this evening. It might work better that way. She peeled off her robe and pulled on a long green dress with a hem which reached the ground. It was perfect for disguising the fact that she would be wearing two different shoes.

The warm slipper fitted her perfectly, just as she'd expected, and on her other foot she wore another with a similar heel. She was ready. Her heart beat fast in her chest. There was no going back now.

Even though she was only wearing one magic slipper, she could see the effect over dinner. Instead of simply casting a bored eye over her before sitting down, this time the prince frowned slightly and then smiled, before coming round to her side of the table and pulling her chair out for her.

'Thank you,' she said.

He leaned down and spoke softly into her ear, his breath tickling the back of her neck. 'You look beautiful tonight.'

She smiled and, when he sat down, lifted her glass to click against his but she only sipped at her drink, even though she longed for the bravery that came with wine. She needed to keep her wits about her for later. The prince, however, drank his.

All through the meal he talked to her, attentive to her every need, asking about how her music lessons were coming and telling her how excited he was for the wedding to come quickly. It was all the conversation Cinderella had wished for when she first came to the castle but now, somehow, although she smiled and laughed in all the right places, it bored her. *He* bored her. She thought of the picture she'd kept on her wall in their old house, how she'd dreamed of meeting her handsome prince and falling in love, and now, as he talked of the hunt and his friends and various balls that were being arranged in their honour, she realised that his personality had about as much depth as that picture.

The king and queen smiled approvingly – if not without a little surprise – at how engaged their son was with his ill-chosen bride and when the meal finally drew to a close the king suggested that perhaps the prince should walk Cinderella back to her apartments. The prince didn't argue and the young couple left the dining room arm in arm.

'I was wondering, your highness,' Cinderella started, her heart racing so hard in her chest that she was sure he must be able to hear it, 'if you still had my other shoe from the ball. I want to wear them with a new dress.'

'Yes, of course I do,' he said, looking down and smiling at her. 'It's in my apartments. We can go there now if you'd like.'

Her stomach came up to her throat as she nodded. There was no turning back now. Why was she suddenly so nervous? He was handsome. She'd wanted him for such a long time. Maybe when she had the other shoe on, all the passion she'd felt at the ball would come back. Maybe if she *kept* the shoes on, he'd love her forever and she'd live happily ever after with a husband who adored her. It was an empty thought. Who really wanted an enchanted love? She hadn't, even before the ball. She'd just presumed they'd fall in love if given the opportunity, as if love was something easy and took nothing but a pretty face and a longing for it to achieve. She realised she felt nothing for him and, in a way, that was worse than if she hated him.

Her mismatched heels clicked down the corridor below her dress as they drew closer and closer to his rooms. His arm pulled her tighter to him; a rare gesture of affection. He was talking softly to her of their future, but it was drowned out by the hum of blood and the thumping of her heart.

A footman with his back to them was polishing the silver arms of a decorative chair just past the prince's door and she suddenly felt an overwhelming urge to talk to him if just to delay stepping inside. She bit the inside of her cheek instead. There was no point in delaying. She needed to get the key and discover the contents of that room. Delaying now wouldn't prevent the inevitable. At least the prince was a little hazy from wine and if everything went well would soon be asleep.

She took a deep breath and stood tall. She was no longer a foolish little girl. She was a woman and it was time to start behaving like one. She'd got herself into this – it was her responsibility to see it through.

The effect was almost instant. He'd retrieved the shoe from the top of the wardrobe and as soon as she'd slipped it onto her other foot she saw the change in his expression. The lights were low in the room and his eyes glazed as he looked at her.

'How could I have forgotten how beautiful you are?' he said softly, more to himself than her as he walked towards her. Her heart thumped as his hand slid round her waist, his arm pulling her tight. She felt as if she couldn't breathe. She lifted one hand and rested it on his arm. It was muscular and firm and his chest was broad and strong. He smelled of light cologne and body heat. His white shirt was unbuttoned at the collar and the patch of skin she could see was pale and hair free. Suddenly, she felt as if she might cry.

'Oh, Cinderella,' he breathed as he slid one hand into her hair and tilted her head back, exactly as the huntsman had done, but this time she felt nothing. His lips lowered to hers and kissed her, gently at first and then, as she felt him becoming aroused and pressing against her, with more urgency.

Her spine stiffened. She waited for the rush of passion she'd felt before, but none came. Instead, she began to squirm in his arms, trying to twist her head away and break their embrace. He held her tighter, mistaking her movements for excitement. His breathing was coming hard and he was lost in his lust.

'No, look...' she started to say as he broke away for air, but then his mouth was on hers again, and one of his hands was tugging at the laces of her dress as he turned her around, moving them towards the bed.

'No, we shouldn't... I don't—'

He wasn't listening to her as he pushed her backwards and started tugging at his trousers. He was murmuring under his breath, no doubt sweet nothings, but Cinderella didn't want to hear them. She no longer cared about the key or the room upstairs, she just wanted to be free of his grip so she could run away and keep on running. She tried to push him off her but he grabbed her arms and held them down with one hand as his mouth moved down her neck and towards her breasts. His other hand reached under her skirt, and he groaned as his fingers felt their way up her leg.

'No, please stop...' Cinderella said again, aware that sobs were beginning to choke her throat. This wasn't what she wanted. This wasn't how she'd thought it would be. She desperately tried to free herself of the charmed shoes, but they were fixed tightly to her feet. She closed her eyes and tried to withdraw into herself as her body continued to struggle against him. His hand reached higher and higher, pushing her skirt up and...

... and then the weight of him was gone as someone hauled him off the bed with a grunt and the prince cried out in surprise. Cinderella looked up dazed, her vision bleary.

'How dare you!' the prince hissed at the footman as the two men faced each other at the end of the bed. The footman punched him hard, sending the prince reeling.

'Shit,' the attacker said and winced, touching his side, before punching the recovering prince again and sending him to the floor clutching his mouth.

Cinderella's eyes widened. This was no ordinary footman. It was the huntsman. *Her* huntsman. She scrabbled to her feet and without even straightening her dress ran to him and flung her arms round his neck. He reeled back slightly and put one hand around her.

'Thank you,' she said, looking up at him. His skin was rough and he smelt of the forest and she felt a rush of warmth tingling through her body.

'You're welcome.' He looked down at her. 'But just so you know, this plan stank.'

'You!' The prince was on his feet, his bottom lip was bleeding. 'I thought you were dead.' His face flushed as his passion mixed with anger.

'You never bothered to find out,' the huntsman said.

Cinderella looked from one to the other. 'You know each other?'

'That's a story for another time,' the huntsman said. He pulled a knife out from under his jacket. 'And now I think we'll take that key around your neck.'

'You'll never get away with this,' the prince hissed. He looked at Cinderella. 'My darling, step away from him. I love you. I—'

'Oh, take those bloody shoes off, woman,' the huntsman cut in. 'We'll never get any sense out of him until you do.' Cinderella did as she was told and the prince's face immediately fell, confused. He stared at her as if he was looking at a stranger.

'What do you want?' he asked. 'What's going on here?'

'You tell us,' the huntsman said, nodding at Cinderella to tie the prince's hands behind his back. She rummaged in the wardrobe and found a grey silk necktie and used that, pulling a tight knot around his wrists. Then she reached around his neck and undid the chain. The gold key hanging there shone brightly.

'Got it,' she said, smiling.

'You can't go into that room,' the prince growled, his face darkening. 'No one knows what's in there. It's mine. It's private.'

'Oh, I think I have a pretty good idea,' the huntsman said, grabbing the prince by his arm and holding him close, the knife pressed under his ribs. 'And private it might be, but it doesn't belong to you.'

'You'll take the Troll Road for this,' the prince snarled. 'You'll—'

Cinderella thrust a screwed up flannel into his mouth turning his words into muted grunts.

'That's better,' she said, and then smiled at the huntsman. 'Shall we?' She picked up the diamond slippers and crept to the door. She peered out. The corridor was empty.

With the knife held firmly so close to his vital organs, the prince didn't struggle but let the huntsman and Cinderella lead him. They crept past her apartments into the darker, quieter core of the castle and then started up the cool winding stairs. The moon was in hiding and the steps were simply ghosts in the darkness beneath her feet. Cinderella's heart thumped in her chest. There was so much she didn't understand. How did the huntsman and the prince know each other? How much did the huntsman know about what was hidden in the room, and why did the fairy godmother want it so badly? And she couldn't help but wonder how to get herself out of a lifetime married to the odious man now snivelling behind his gag, snot running from his nose.

All her wondering stopped as the huntsman froze just as they rounded last corner. He raised his hand and she stopped where she stood. Her scalp prickled as she stared into the black musty space. She didn't need to ask him what was wrong. She could sense it herself. They weren't alone up here. Beside her, the huntsman was tense, ready to spring into attack, and then, from deep within the gloom came the delicate tap of silver on stone.

'I wondered when you'd get here.'

'Rose?' Cinderella said, incredulous as her step-sister came into view. 'What are you doing here?'

'I followed your markings. I thought something strange

was going on and you might need my help.' She rested her cane against the wall and lit the small lamp in her hand. As she held it up, casting yellow light on the three figures in front of her, she raised an eyebrow. 'I was right on the first count at least.' She dropped into a slight curtsey. 'Your highness.' She looked at Cinderella. 'What the hell is going on?'

The prince was staring at her and his mewling grew louder and more indignant.

'It's a long story,' Cinderella said. 'He's got something secret in that room. And we need it.'

'Come on,' the huntsman pushed the prince forward. 'Let's get this done, shall we?'

Rose held the light up and Cinderella darted forward with the key.

'Are you sure you want to do this, little sister?' Rose asked. 'You're going to be a royal princess. Sometimes you have to look the other way.'

'I can't do that.' Cinderella shook her head. 'And I'm not sure I'm going to be a royal princess either.' Just saying the words aloud made her feel better, as if a weight had been pressing down on her, pushing her into the very foundations of the castle, and she'd suddenly been freed.

'Oh, Cinders,' Rose said. 'You do like to make life difficult. Go on, then. Unlock the door.'

And Cinderella did.

12

'There has to be a wedding...'

For a moment Cinderella couldn't breathe. She had expected the room to be as dusty and dirty as the rest of this part of the castle, but instead everything shone. The polished floor was inlaid with mosaics of dragons dancing in the summer sky. Overhead a chandelier glittered brightly, rubies and emeralds and diamonds sparkling with the light within. Heavy red velvet drapes hung over the windows and in the corner a table was laden with bottles of wine and a silver goblet. A chaise longue of gold and blue was on the far side of the room, matching cushions at its head and feet as if someone spent a lot of time on it and wanted to be comfortable.

But it was the centrepiece she couldn't tear her eyes from.

'I had no idea what to expect,' Rose said, softly. 'But it wasn't that.'

The glass coffin sat on a raised dais in the middle of the room. Inside it, a beautiful dark-haired girl in a pink dress lay perfectly still. Her cheeks had a dusky rose tint and her lips were cherry red. Cinderella peered in. The girl had the most extraordinary violet eyes. They stared, empty of expression, at the ceiling.

'Snow White,' the huntsman said. 'I knew it.'

Cinderella looked at him. 'You know her?'

'We... we've met.'

'Met?' There was something in his voice that sent a flare of jealousy through her. 'What do you mean, *met*?'

'Her step-mother too as it happens.' He smiled at her, his eyes twinkling and she realised he was enjoying her reaction. 'I was feeling lucky to be alive. And they were hard to resist.' He winked at her and she almost growled again, but swallowed it down. He was *still* infuriating. Was that all their moment had been? Another notch nearly carved on his bedstead?

'You slept with her?' The prince spat his gag out and glared. '*You?*' He looked from the huntsman to Cinderella and back again. 'And her?'

'Not yet. I'm working on it.'

'Don't hold your breath,' Cinderella muttered. The girl in the casket was truly beautiful. She almost looked as if she was just sleeping, but that couldn't be possible.

'If perhaps we could worry less about who's been sleeping with whom, and focus on what's going on here, I think we might make more progress towards a solution.' Rose said, pouring herself a glass of wine. 'I take it this is something to do with how you managed to get to those Bride Balls in dresses you certainly couldn't afford.'

'I made this stupid deal...' Cinderella started. 'I'm so sorry, she gave me these slippers...'

'There's this queen,' the huntsman said, over Cinderella, 'and after he abandoned me she wanted me to kill this girl and I didn't so she cursed me but now...'

'I can explain' the prince joined in.

'Okay, enough!' Rose held her hand up and Cinderella fell silent. She was surprised to see that the huntsman did too. Rose had always been good at being in charge. 'I don't want to get lost in the details. I'm not sure I even want to hear the details.' She looked at the prince.

'Is she dead?'

'No,' he shook his head like a berated child, and Cinderella wondered how she could have ever thought he would be the one for her. He was charming and handsome, but so weak. She looked at the girl in the box. And clearly damaged.

'She's just enchanted.'

'Just,' the huntsman muttered.

'And I take it the king doesn't know she's here?' Rose continued. The prince shook his head.

'He wouldn't understand. I don't *do* anything. I just like to talk to her,' he said, as if it was the most reasonable thing in the world. 'She's so perfect like this. She listens.' He looked at Rose as if she of all of them would understand. 'I wasn't hurting anyone. Not until *he* came back.' He glared at the huntsman. 'I'll have you arrested for this. The Troll Road is too good for you. I'll hang you from the castle walls to rot!' His face had twisted into a sneer and his eyes were cold and ugly.

'And I in turn,' the huntsman leaned casually against the wall, 'will tell your father and anyone who'll listen exactly what happened with that *other* beauty of yours.'

The prince's eyes widened. Cinderella wished she knew what they were talking about. What other beauty? A different girl to the one trapped in the glass box? She stared at her again. Who was this Snow White? She frowned as a glint of gold caught her eye.

'She's wearing a wedding ring,' she said, staring at the frozen girl's left hand. 'She's married.' The truth hit her like a blast of the winter wind and she turned to the prince, her mouth half open. 'She's your *wife*?'

'But that can't be right,' the huntsman said. 'No priest would marry a girl in this condition. No matter who wanted...' his sentence drifted away. 'You bastard,' he said, eventually. 'I knew you were spoilt and pathetic, but this?' His words contained the growl of every predator in the forest, and as he stepped forward the prince cowered backwards, seeking protection from Rose. 'You married her and then did this to her?'

'It wasn't like that,' the prince said, although from the tone of his voice Cinderella was pretty sure it was something close. 'I just... she was just...' his shoulders slumped and whatever energy he had for the fight left him in a heavy sigh. 'I just don't understand beautiful women. They're so much...' he glanced at the glass coffin and then at Cinderella. 'Trouble.'

'I think this cancels our engagement,' Cinderella said.

'But there has to be a wedding! My father will insist on it. All the preparations have been made! I can't tell him about this. I can't...'

'No one's going to tell him about this.' Rose laid a gentle hand on the prince's arm. 'But nor can this continue. It's time to let the past go.' She looked at the huntsman. 'You have someone waiting for this girl?'

He nodded. 'Yes.'

'I'll go with him,' Cinderella blurted out. 'I don't want to live here. And I want to see this queen who's messed with us all so much. And...' she closed her mouth. And what? What had she been about to say? And she couldn't imagine never seeing the huntsman again? She could feel him looking at her and her face burned.

'But there has to be a wedding,' the prince muttered. 'There has to be.'

'And there will be,' Rose said. 'You'll marry me. I'll smooth all this over and the kingdom will carry on happily.'

'Marry you?' He frowned slightly.

'I'll be a good queen,' she said firmly. 'I can guide you through the parts of ruling that you'll find dull. And I won't care when you take mistresses so long as you treat me with the respect a queen deserves.' She held his face until his eyes focused on her. 'It could be a good partnership.'

Slowly, the prince nodded. 'Yes,' he said. 'Thank you.'

'Are you sure?' Cinderella looked at Rose, even though she could feel the rightness of the match in her stomach. Things were as they would have been if she hadn't turned up with her enchanted slippers and wrecked it all.

'Certain,' her step-sister – her *sister* – said. 'I'll explain to mother and father. But you'd better stay in touch. Come and visit when things have calmed down.' She clapped her hands together and smiled. 'Now, we'd better organise you two a cart of some kind. You'll want to be gone before everyone wakes up. And you'll need to dress down.' She lifted her chin and as she walked away, leaning so carefully on her cane, Cinderella thought Rose looked every inch the queen already. Cinderella rummaged in the pockets of her dress and pulled out the final nut the fairy godmother had given her. Escape, that's what she'd said, and Cinderella knew this was exactly the moment she had meant.

13

'Of course it's love...'

Rose was ruthlessly efficient and, by her side, the prince did exactly what he was told. Horses were saddled and a donkey brought out of the stables and attached to the cart.

'He looks old and tired,' the prince muttered. 'But he'll walk steadily and for as long as you need him to.' He looked at the girl in the glass coffin on the back of the cart. 'If she wakes up, she'll know who he belongs to.' He didn't look at Cinderella as she flung a small bag of possessions alongside it, and she didn't care. She had nothing to say to him. Neither did the huntsman, or so it seemed. He looked pained. 'Hurry up,' he told her. 'I haven't... we haven't got a lot of time.'

She nodded. Rose came alongside her and pushed a small bag in her hand. It was heavy with coins. 'I can't take that,'

Cinderella protested. 'Not after everything. I'm so sorry. You were right. I was spoilt. Stupid.'

Rose pulled her in tight and hugged her. 'No. Everything is as it should be. And all will be well.' She stroked Cinderella's face and smiled. 'You'll see. Now go before I get too emotional.'

The moon broke through the heavy clouds as they slipped away but when Cinderella looked back Rose was still standing by the gates. She raised her hand, and Cinderella did the same, just before cracking the nut and letting the dust settle over her and the huntsman. She breathed in, and her fine court gown turned into a dusty green dress. It was the colour of the forest and she loved it. Once her sister was out of sight, she kept her head down. This city held nothing for her anymore.

They travelled in relative silence until they reached the edge of the sleeping city and the border of the snowy forest, disappearing under its canopy and being embraced by the trees. The huntsman led them to a track and gave her his jacket to keep warm. Slowly dawn was edging into the sky, bringing a strange light with it that found gaps in the branches and cut strange shapes around them. Cinderella noticed that the huntsman was pale and trembling. Was it his injuries? Or was he about to transform back into the tiny mouse? She touched his arm. 'Are you all right?' she asked.

He nodded, but his face was drawn and his eyes were filled with sadness. 'You might have to finish this journey alone,' he said, and glanced up at the sky, his handsome face furrowing.

'Well, only until tonight,' Cinderella said. 'I'll keep you warm until you become a man again.'

He shook his head. 'I don't think it will be that way this time. The deal changed.'

'What do you mean?' Cinderella stared at him. He had to be joking. 'She can't do that.'

'Have you got the slippers? She'll want them back.'

'Yes,' Cinderella was still staring at him. 'They're in my bag.' She thought of all the times they'd laughed in the doorway by the kitchen. She thought of how he'd saved her from the prince. She thought— suddenly a whole new thought struck her. The slippers.

'Why didn't the slippers work on you?' she said. 'When you came in the prince's room? They didn't affect you at all.'

He smiled, creases forming around his eyes, and he looked at her. His dark hair hung over one eye, but she could still see all the kindness and strength and warmth that lay beneath his humour and roughness. 'They didn't work on me because I dreamt of you before we met,' he said simply. 'And there's no magic stronger than that.' He looked away and moved his horse forward.

'You love me?' she said. The cold was forgotten. Her head was in a whirl. Love? Is that what this was? All this irritation? All this infuriating anger?

You're on a dirt track in the freezing forest at dawn. You've left your family behind without a second thought.

Of course it's love.

'Wait,' she called after him, jumping down from her horse, her heart racing with joy. He turned and looked at her. His trembling was getting worse. He was changing and she couldn't allow that to happen, not without letting him know. She ran to him and he slid from his saddle, his legs almost buckling under him as he stood.

'Don't watch this,' he said. He gasped and bent over a little. 'Please.'

Cinderella took his face in her hands. Her whole body tingled just from touching him.

'I love you too,' she whispered. And then she kissed him.

She wasn't sure if it was just inside her head, but she was sure that as he held her, the stars danced around their heads and lights twinkled in a whirlwind of fireflies that warmed their hands. She was lost in the moment and so was he.

'The curse,' he said, pulling back slightly. 'You broke the curse.'

'I don't care what I did,' Cinderella murmured. 'Just kiss me again.'

His lips met hers and as their tongues danced together, their bodies wound around each other's, he pulled her down to the forest floor. For a moment, caught up by the magic of true love, the forest created a space of warmth for them. The ice evaporated and the earth welcomed them. Cinderella ran her fingers through his dark hair and this time there were no comparisons with the prince's blond good looks. They were sterile. This man was all passion and nature. Panting as his hands pulled at her clothes, she reached between them and tugged at his belt. This time he didn't stop her, pushing her dress upwards and groaning slightly as her hand found him. Cinderella thrust her hips up to him, aching to finally feel him inside her, already warm and wet and wanting. There would be time for exploring each other later. There would be time for everything later. For now there was only urgency, all of the delayed need between them. He pushed inside her and she gasped, wrapping her legs around his hips, pulling him in further as he moved, one hand touching the roughness of his face and the other sliding down between them and touching herself. She didn't care about princes and shoes or fairy godmothers and curses. This was all the magic they needed.

When they were done they lay there for a while, talking quietly and laughing and kissing until need overwhelmed them again, but this time it was slow and controlled and their mouths went where their hands had been before and when the gentleness was done and she was sure they were both going to explode from it, they took each other again.

* * *

It was late afternoon when they reached the boundary between kingdoms and found the fairy godmother waiting for them. Her long blonde hair hung loose around her shoulders and she wore riding breeches under her thick fur coat. A carriage sat patiently in the road further back.

She turned to Cinderella, her expression hard to read in the encroaching gloom. 'I see you realised the prince wasn't the hero of your dreams after all.' She smiled, and it was almost gentle. 'I think you made the better choice.' She walked round to the back of the cart, pausing to pat the donkey's neck.

The sun broke through in streaks of reds and pinks leaving the sky stained as if with blood as the queen or fairy godmother or whoever she was stared into the back of the cart.

'I'll take it from here,' she said.

With her hair loose around her pale cat-like features, Cinderella didn't think the woman looked like a queen or a fairy godmother at all. She looked like a water witch from the legends her step-mother used to read to her, tales from the days of the dragons. She didn't know whether to be afraid or in awe. Probably both.

'And it will be as you said?' the huntsman asked.

The queen nodded.

'Let's go,' the huntsman muttered. 'I'm done here.'

Cinderella thought of her huntsman cursed to become a mouse. She thought of the girl in the box and wondered how that story would end. She turned her horse around though, and as they rode away, leaving the icy queen and the frozen girl behind, she decided that for her that story was done. She had her own story to live. She looked at the handsome man beside her and smiled, before spurring her horse into a canter and heading into the woods.

14

'Is that a spindle...?'

Rose had dyed her hair red for the wedding, and she found it suited her as well as fooling just about everyone that the prince was still marrying the same girl. After all, who had really paid any attention to Cinderella? The people had only seen her from a distance, and anyone in the court who might have realised something rather strange had gone on – that the girl walking down the aisle was taller and more buxom than the curly-haired beauty they'd trained to walk and dance – knew well enough to keep their mouths firmly shut. The prince was married and that was all anyone needed to know.

She was content. She had never wanted love in the way that other girls sought it out. For some, love was needed for life; it kept their hearts racing with its ups and downs and desire for one person to make you complete. Rose had always felt complete, and what she wanted was to shape things. To make the kingdom better. The prince would be a good husband in his own way and as time passed she knew she would come to make most of the important decisions. It would work better for them both that way.

She looked out of the window and down to the courtyard below where lights still glittered in the trees and in the bushes of the maze beyond. There had been a sudden thaw, and although it was only just approaching the New Year spring had been in the air for the three days of festivities that had accompanied the royal wedding.

A figure standing in one of the maze paths caught her eye. He stood perfectly still, wearing a bright crimson jacket, and staring up at their bedroom window as if he could see her looking back, which she was sure was impossible. She frowned. What a strange man.

'Darling,' she murmured to the prince, who was changing his shirt for their dinner with the high council and king, 'come and look at this. There's a man in the maze.' She squinted, trying to focus more closely. 'What's that on his back?' He was carrying some kind of knapsack, but there was something sticking out of it. 'Is that a spindle?'

The prince came alongside her.

'Oh no,' he said, his reflection in the glass pale as his eyes widened. 'I didn't think he'd find me.'

Rose's heart sank a little. 'What did you do?'

'I made a deal,' the prince said.

He was still talking but Rose wasn't listening. She stared at the stranger, who stared directly back. She drew herself up tall and then took her handsome husband's hand.

'We'll take care of it, dear,' she said. 'The thing about deals, you see, is that they can always be renegotiated.'

Perhaps her married life was going to be more interesting than she'd thought.

'Why don't you tell me what happened?'

EPILOGUE

'**T**rue love's kiss...'

When the sound of hooves had faded the queen climbed up on to the cart and stared at the silent girl on the other side of the glass. 'I just need to know,' she whispered, before carefully opening the glass lid.

The forest was eerily still around them, as if even the winter wolves were holding their breaths.

Her heart raced as she leaned over the thin glass edge and pressed her lips against Snow White's. They were warm and soft, and Lilith thought her heart might stop in that instant of sweetness. She thought of the cabinet where her own face would stare back from the enchanted mirror. She thought of the words it used to speak, tormenting her with the honesty of her innermost truths, ones she'd fought to deny for so long. She'd fought them for so long she'd confused love for hate.

'Snow White, the fairest in all the lands.'

And she was. Beautiful, kind and desirable.

The girl in the box gasped, life flooding back to her violet eyes, and the sun burst through the clouds creating a rainbow above their heads. The queen sat back on her heels as the girl slowly took in her surroundings and sat up.

'I'm so sorry,' Lilith said, eventually. They were inadequate words. But what else could she say. Her heart raced. She had her answer and it was one she should have seen so long ago.

'I thought you hated me,' Snow White said. 'I only ever wanted you to love me.'

They stared at each other for a long moment, and then Snow White reached out and pulled the queen forwards, kissing her again.

When they finally broke for air, they sat and smiled and Lilith thought of the wisdom of her great grandmother's curses. True love was the only true magic. The huntsman had earned his happiness. Just as she hoped they had earned theirs.

'Let's go home,' she said, taking Snow White by the hand and helping her down from the dwarves' cart.

The dark haired beauty paused and smiled. 'Are you wearing riding breeches?' She slid her arm around the woman's waist and they were a vision of light and dark and winter melted around them.

'How did you wake me?' she said.

'True love's kiss,' the queen answered and the two beautiful women smiled at each other. 'We should go home. We'll pick up my great-grandmother on the way. I think she's been causing a bit of trouble. She can go without children for a while.'

'Children?' Snow White asked.

'Oh, you'll understand when you see her house,' the queen said. 'But I should probably apologise for her in advance.'

'I'm sure I'll love her.'

And then they kissed again.

THE END

ABOUT THE AUTHOR

Sarah Pinborough is a critically acclaimed horror, thriller and YA author. She has written for *New Tricks* on the BBC and has an original horror film in development. Sarah won the British Fantasy Award for Best Novella with *Beauty* in 2013, Best Short Story in 2009, and has three times been short-listed for Best Novel. She has also been short-listed for a World Fantasy Award.

www.sarahpinborough.com

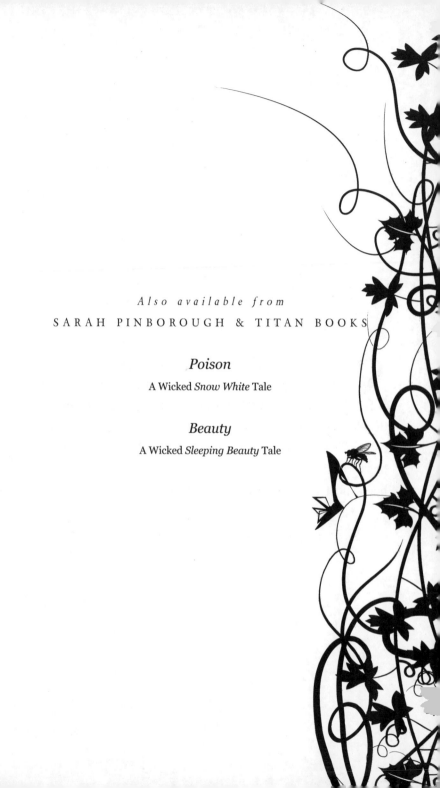

Also available from

SARAH PINBOROUGH & TITAN BOOKS

Poison

A Wicked *Snow White* Tale

Beauty

A Wicked *Sleeping Beauty* Tale